The Adventurer

A Western Novel

Richard G. Hole

Far West

SYNOPSIS

For a couple of months, the streets of San Francisco were a tragic battlefield.

The gunmen dedicated themselves to looking for their weakest rivals in the business and hunting them as best they could, and at that time the city's cemetery was a pilgrimage of coffins that had to wait rigorously for their turn to give them the opportunity to provide them with a space to rest in a once forever ...

The Adventurer is a story belonging to the Far West collection, a collection of novels developed in the American Wild West.

THE ADVENTURER

CHAPTER I

ARMISTICE MANAGEMENT

San Francisco, the pearl of the Pacific, vibrated with exaltation, with unusual joy, with people attacked by the highest fever; it was like a colossal madhouse, so big that madmen seemed to be loose in it, when in fact they were locked in that exotic patch of wild coastline.

Those were the exalted times when gold, being the lever of the world, could be assured that it was worthless because of its abundance, and yet people fought and coldly killed each other to possess it and the most daring men of the four cardinal points , they came to San Francisco attracted by its splendor and by the easy way to win it, provided that it was understood as easy to possess a hard heart, a suicidal impetuosity and an agile and cultivated hand wielding the colt.

With these elements it was possible to live splendidly and treasure the yellow metal; Anyone who had "killed his man," and by killing a man meant having dramatically suppressed a rival as dangerous as himself, had the absolute franchise to be the owner of whatever he wanted. The personal value of individuals was quoted the same as gold, and although there were many who aspired to become a good stock tradable in that tough market, every day they fell in droves, because their excess of them would have made life impossible for them. others.

The main street of San Francisco, long thoroughfare, heart and brain of the city, Third Street and some others of outstanding importance were full of sumptuous and striking premises, where gold flowed as in an overflowing melting pot. Anyone who had made a good poster and intended to exploit it without running excessive avatars to earn money, used to establish a bar or a gambling den, sure that alcohol, the cheerful and easy-going girls who served as bait and the gaming tables would fill their pockets, with no more logical expositions than those derived from the exploitation of vice.

But there came a time when those who understood the business differently, weighing the issue, considered that the profits of gambling den owners and gamblers were excessive for what they risked, and their sharp wit established a new mode of exploitation of the people.

The method was to impose a daily fee on all the premises, in exchange for which they would allow them to continue exploiting their customers without a third dangerous intervention by the inventors.

It is true that there were rebellions to allow themselves to be subjugated in that comfortable way, but a few mass assaults, some arson and two or three murders of recalcitrant owners to pay the tribute somewhat tamed the nerves of the others and all, accepting the least evil. , they chose to pay that strange contribution.

Not with this the conflict was resolved. A new one emerged from it, which was to define who had the "right" to collect the fee.

Each gunman with some strength assumed this right and there came a time when the fleeced, seeing themselves in constant harassment by some and by others, and fearing that not even with the total profits they would obtain enough to cover so many mouths, they decided to put I curb abuse, refusing to pay through thick and thin.

It was already good that one "the strongest" participated in their benefits as a compensation to allow them to obtain them, but not eight or ten, which made the cow something so flaccid that it was not going to give of itself to anyone.

It was then that Konny Foot and Michel Fritt, the two boldest and best organized of all the gunmen, decided to put some order in that chaos that was sapping their profits. If the product was distributed among many, it would be scarce, and since it was no longer the hostility of the owners of the gambling dens, but the competition between those of the same litter, they decided to start clearing their path of obstacles.

For a couple of months, the streets of the city were a tragic battlefield. Both, separately, dedicated themselves to looking for their weakest rivals in the business and hunting them as best they could, and at that time the San Francisco cemetery was a pilgrimage of coffins that had to wait rigorously for their turn to give them the opportunity to provide them with a hole where stand once and for all.

The cleanup was so bloody that the few who were left to continue the battle realized it was suicide to continue. They were the least and least powerful, and of their own free will they withdrew from the competition, dedicating themselves to promoting their income by other means no less reprehensible, but which did not touch the fiefdom of the two gunmen.

And so a day came when only Foot and Fritt stood face to face.

They were both strong, daring and tough, and both had elements, rough and hardened to support them; then the fight became more tragic and more complicated, because both of them knew the terrain they were treading and what the enemy in front of them was worth.

But as the self-esteem of each one was going to feel hurt if it gave way after many successes, to resolve the situation they decided to undertake a fight of colossi, and using all kinds of cunning and daring blows they tried to eliminate themselves.

But the matter was not as easy to resolve as it seemed. There were many casualties on both sides "casualties that each one rushed to cover immediately" because there was never a lack of elements willing to be part of the band to live well, and therefore, despite the casualties, nothing was achieved to incline the balance in favor of one of the two bosses, until both, who were not stupid, thought that the time was coming to parley and seek an advantageous solution, but that would not leave them in a ridiculous situation.

It was Foot who thought about it first, and after thinking about it and exchanging impressions with his most prominent men, he decided to test the waters.

It was not a very viable undertaking to contact his rival. The two feared each other and both took drastic precautions so as not to give the other the facility to eliminate him, and for this reason something had to be invented that would put them in contact without immediate danger and without suspicion when conducting the interview.

Then Foot thought of the best person to arrange the interview. This person was Agnes Desher, "California Beauty," as the bronze people of San Francisco called her. A blonde of provocative and attractive beauty, a woman already curdled in life and with a fortitude worthy of the toughest gunman, since she had rolled through all the mining fields, and by dint of skill, of knowing how to exploit her beauty and not feeling scruples to win money, he had raised quite an excellent capital, which enabled him to establish a magnificent gambling den on the street of San Francisco, which was attended by the best and most turbulent of the city.

Agnes, skillful, had managed to capture the friendship of both leaders. The two threatened her at first, they both demanded a large sum from her for letting her live in peace and exploit the gambling den at her pleasure, and she had tamed both of them, getting her to stay out of all tribute as an exception.

Nobody knew about the kind of trickery that she appealed to to achieve it, and only she mattered, but Agnes, a practical and suggestive woman, had hinted more than once that this was not the best procedure to solve the conflict, since they would live in perpetual war biting his own tail without reaching anything definite.

The two used to visit her a few times. It was true that when they did, they appeared well guarded by the cream of their guardians, fearing to run into their rival, and both felt a special attraction for that energetic and brave woman, who disdaining their sex and endowed with an aggressiveness Extraordinary, she hadn't been afraid to settle in the roughest and wildest city in all of California, exploiting, in addition, the roughest and most compromising business imaginable.

In their conversations with Agnes, the two of them had been irreducible. Their vanity as gunmen could not compromise with a denigrating pact, because they had lost face with their men and this was more dangerous than suffering a shooting defeat in the middle of the street. But, as circumstances demanded, Foot felt that he should listen to Agnes's advice and consult with her. Her power, her attraction and her cunning as a woman were weapons that, when well wielded, could do much to resolve the conflict.

So one night, surrounded by his six best men, Foot showed up at the gambling den. It was crowded with miners, gamblers, livelihoods, people of high rank in the town, and to top it off, enlivened by a chorus of pretty and provocatively dressed girls, who were the best hook that "the Californian Beauty" could put on her fishing line. fish customers.

And for this, Agnes's somewhat autumnal beauty should not be overlooked. This was a very good-looking blonde, still with a smooth and well-made-up face, the owner of a pair of large, deep black eyes that knew how to play with mischief or naivety, as it suited her to disarm the most determined in front of her, and She was endowed with a slender and well-groomed body, which she enhanced with wisely tailored dresses toned in color, cut to better enhance her person, and also possessed a collection of valuable and eye-catching jewels that gleamed in the light of the oil lamps, making her more eye-catching. its silhouette.

A rare thing in a city as rough and bustling as that one; only once did someone, a little mistaken, try to appropriate his jewelry box. Taking advantage of a carelessness, he managed to slip into Agnes's private rooms, where he hid himself determined not to leave without the coveted loot.

She must have suspected something or something she had invented to know if someone entered her private rooms, because when she retired to them quietly and without asking for the help of the men she had at her service to guard the premises, she armed herself with the two small revolvers which he always kept hidden in his pockets and pushed the door open with his foot stepping aside.

When the intruder, believing that Agnes was entering, stepped forward with a revolver in hand to intimidate her, she found herself without knowing how with two ounces of lead on her chest. Properly directed, the thief only lasted long enough to realize the mistake he had made, since five minutes later he was in a position to appear in the mortuary census of the town.

But Agnes was a very refined woman, and she was not content to calmly and courageously eliminate danger. He needed to make it public and launch an alarm call to those like that one who might be too dazzled by the shine of his jewels, and calling the most trusted man he had in the gambling den, he ordered:

"Billy, carry that carrion and take it to where you find a tree with strong branches. Hang him on it and put this paper on his chest for those who are curious to know it to read.

The paper said briefly:

"She was killed by Agnes Desher, 'California Beauty', for trying to steal her jewelry by raiding her rooms."

The ad was healthy. The Golden Herald, the city's most widely circulated newspaper, picked up the story and commented on it to its liking. Agnes was an institution in San Francisco and everything that affected her interested both the neighborhood and the floating population.

The event was commented on in all tones and in all gambling dens and recreational venues, and, as she claimed, it was a forceful warning that prevented her from new temptations to plunder.

This was the intermediary Foot had chosen to resolve his differences with Fritt. If she wanted "and was sure she would", she could arrange the interview with her rival on neutral ground, where neither would have to fear the other.

That night Agnes was in her glory. The tables were working at full capacity, the counter bar was packed with customers who drank without tax, and the other tables that occupied the center of the joint were occupied by an audience so crowded that they barely had space to move, and by If that was not enough, the state senator had felt happy visiting the joint and gallantly courting its owner, despite being a man in his sixties and paunchy, dominated by asthma and somewhat clumsy when walking due to his severe attacks of rheumatism.

But the senator was a somewhat theoretical power, but a power in San Francisco, and Agnes did not disdain to flatter him and go along with him, sure that at any moment of need she would make him go head over heels for her benefit.

When he saw Foot appear, he smiled expressively, showing between the painted red of his lips the immaculate snow of his fine and well-cared teeth.

Motioning him to come forward, he indicated the table that he always had reserved for his friends, and Foot, going forward, ordered his men to keep watch and at the same time not lose sight of him.

Agnes sat next to the gunman, commenting:

Hello, Foot. I have not seen your cute mustache for more than three weeks. That is a humiliation for my suggestive person and I will have to complain against you. Are you so busy sending people to hell that you don't have time to visit a good friend, or are you ... afraid to go out because of the cold of the night?

"A little bit of everything, Agnes, why should I deny it? "Replied the gunman smiling cynically." You know the weather in San Francisco well and you know that, at certain times, particularly at night, it is not very healthy. My precious health is very demanding.

"What use are all those good-looking guys who accompany you as your shadow?

"Oh! Against a hurricane of lead arising in the shadows of the night, all clothing is insufficient. The Empire of Shadows is great, but it has its drawbacks as well.

"It's true. So how dare you come tonight?

"Because I need to talk to you.

She, staring at him, replied:

"It will not be to resurrect that of the operating canon or to repeat to me again that you like me, that you would form a partnership with me and even that you would take me to New York to live as an oriental princess. That is already well spent, Foot.

"Shut up that viper's tongue, Agnes," replied the gunman. You know that you are my weakness and I excluded you from the payment of benefits. As for the other, I have given up on repeating it to you because I have convinced myself that you are too green a fruit to nail the tooth.

Despite the fact that some spiteful assure that I am already too mature?

"Good. There are fruits that when they begin to ripen give a feeling of hardness and you are one of those. But let's get this matter down to the point. I have something more important to talk to you about.

"Don't disappoint me, Foot! "She assured making a mischievous gesture of spite." For a woman who aspires to always have men on their knees and at their feet, that is an insult. What is it about?

"I would like to speak with you quietly," Foot assured, glancing around them. " I need to expose you an idea that I have been maturing and I need your advice.

"Ah! Women who look young, but are old, usually have enough life experience to advise beardless toddlers like you, don't we, Foot?

"Don't be scathing, Agnes," Foot replied. Your instinct and your wisdom have nothing to do with your age, but with what you have lived and seen. I have not been wrong in anything that refers to you.

Except for making love to me. You know that this is a microbe that does not find a place to prey on my beautiful person.

"Don't claim victory in spite of everything. If one day it finds a loophole to stick its poison in you, that day you will be lost.

"That's why I disinfect myself daily. Here, this is the key to my rooms. As I am not afraid of criticism, go up to the gallery, open up and wait for me there. In a while I'll be by your side to listen to you.

He gave her a loving pat on the face and got up. Foot approached one of his men, exchanged a few words in a low voice with him, and disappeared down the regal staircase that, opening in two branches to the right and left, led to the gallery.

His bodyguards stood guard near the staircase and Agnes, after chatting with the senator, who had decided to put a few dollars on the roulette wheel, went up to look for the gunman.

He was waiting for her, lying indolently on a divan dock next to a small table where he found a bottle of whiskey and cigarettes. The soft light of a lamp hung from the ceiling cast its reflections squarely on Boot's face, while his revolver radiated metallic reflections, placed almost next to the bottle and within the fastest reach of his hand.

Agnes took a deep look at him, trying to encompass with her gaze everything she could read in the sparkling black eyes of the savage gunman, that man with harmonious lines, flexible waist and serene face, who was one of the greatest powers in San Francisco.

And this time she found him different from others. Now he looked like a tired and aged man. His eyes, always cheerful and a bit mocking, retained the same brightness, a feverish glow, like a hardness of radiance that denounced him as a hard man that he was, but deep wrinkles were marked on his forehead, perhaps of worries, if not it was scary, and the corners of his thin lips were sketched in slight folds that seemed to have put three or four more years on him than he had.

But they were only details seen through the inquisitive gaze of a shrewd and overly observant woman. Apart from these details, he was still the virile, strong, flexible and tough man, in his full vigor, who continued to maintain the hegemony that he proposed to achieve in the town, when a year ago he arrived astray as one of many and that by courage, fierceness and cunning managed to become the leader of one of the most fearsome bands of the pearl of the Pacific.

He had lit a cigar and his glass of whiskey was half full. Agnes cheekily sat opposite him in a provocative attitude and exclaimed wryly:

"What happens to the baby from San Francisco who needs the advice of Mom Agnes? Speak up, doll, and tell mom who makes you suffer.

He ignored the spicy jokes of "California Beauty" and replied:

"I have come to see you because I have been pondering your advice, Agnes.

"Too terrible an effort for your intellect, which will have given you many headaches. What are you talking about? I have given you many more than a loving mother, but you are so yours that you have always despised them. What happens now that you have been forced to meditate late?

"It's about Fritt.

"Ah! Things are not going very well for both of us. It is not like this?

"Do not. They are not going well, or at least I think so. This does not mean that neither of us has gained a decisive step over the other, but I understand that we are running out and reducing our strength with positive losses without deciding the fight, and this has to end sometime.

"How?

"I don't know and it's what I need to know. If we are both a positive force that we cannot eliminate each other, we have to do something to end it.

"And what do you think you can do?

"Agree on a good arrangement.

"Wow! That already came out. How much time have you lost to convince yourself?

"Quite a lot, that's why I'd like to try another way. I do not know if Fritt will be convinced that it is the most convenient and I want to know. That's why I came to talk to you.

"What is your idea, Foot?

"A very simple one. You have as much friendship with him as with me. Try to probe him to see what his predisposition is for reaching a compromise. If you think, as I do, that the time has come to fix us, let's fix it.

"If not?

"If not ... well ... I think I will risk everything to a card looking for him as it is so that we finish one of the two.

"It would be a nice ending after so much fighting that the two of you eliminated, although I don't think so. What should I do?

"I do not know. Give me a solution.

"I will try to help you because I appreciate you both. I'm going to have Fritt come and talk to him. If I see you in favor of an arrangement, I will organize a dinner and meet you with me right here. You will speak under the surveillance of my revolvers, and if anyone tries to take advantage of my friendly intervention for more than just talking, they will have to count on me.

"For my part, I promise to respect your neutrality.

"I trust your word. Do you have a solution in mind?

"Do not. I will have to do it. I wasn't sure ...

"It does not matter. Study him while I study something, and if he brings his ideas too, maybe something acceptable will come out.

"Will you warn him that the three of us will meet?

"Do not. I do not want to expose myself to coming with people willing to do more than argue. I will surprise him with the invitation, but I beg you to be prudent.

"Don't worry, I will.

"In that case, I think there is no more to talk about this matter for now. I will send you a message announcing the night and time of the meeting.

He stood up flexible and agile, saying:

"I am very grateful to you, Agnes. You're a wonderful woman. That's why you became interested in me, because a man like me needs a woman like you.

"But I don't need those complications. My independence is so wild that I doubt there is a man who can take it. If there were ... I think it would show me as much in love with him as a schoolgirl.

They both laughed at the statement and he, coming closer, dared to kiss her. Agnes stated:

"Don't get your hopes up about this. It is a commodity that I lavish and not that is spent, but it means nothing. Take care when retiring, the night air is very bad.

And he went down with him to the hall to deliver it to his guards.

CHAPTER II

PEACE TREATY

Two days later, Foot received notice from "La Bella Californiana" so that that night at ten o'clock she would report to the joint. He recommended that he enter directly through the adjoining door, independent of the main one, and go directly to their rooms, gaining the ladder that led to them.

He also recommended that he discreetly remove his men and not show up a minute before the appointed time.

Foot did not hold back any ambush from Agnes. He thought he knew her well to know her loyal, apart from the fact that he was personally interested in being so.

Fritt, in turn, had received the same invitation, but for half an hour earlier. She did not want the two men to meet before she could control them, since Fritt ignored the maneuvers of his competitor and the owner of the joint.

Fritt was very puzzled by the invitation, but he knew of Agnes's somewhat unrepentant nature and of her interest in getting along with him. For this reason, he replied that he agreed to dine in his company and that he would come at the time set.

When Fritt arrived at the gambling den, and by the same path indicated to his rival, he reached the private rooms of "La Bella Californiana," he felt somewhat puzzled. A sumptuous table was set with clean white tablecloths, gleaming china, and clear crystal goblets. Agnes, after greeting him friendly, indicated a seat and he commented:

"Are you celebrating your birthday, Agnes?

"No, honey. That is a date that I try to forget as much as I can. The years are the only enemy that I fear and I try to forget that it exists.

"So, this intimate dinner, what does it obey?

"A lot of things that I find interesting, Fritt. I never do things to do them without a justified purpose. Sit down and help yourself to something, we won't be long in starting dinner.

He sank into a comfortable chair and poured himself whiskey. Agnes glanced at him to try to guess his reactions, but Fritt was a hermetic and cold man, in whose eyes it was always very difficult to read what he was thinking.

He was a very attractive guy as a man. Tall and flexible, he wore with refined elegance his wide hazel-colored frock coat, his fancy waistcoat crossed at the chest by a thick gold chain, his white silk shirt, impeccable, with a large maroon ceiling and in the center a huge diamond in the middle. horseshoe shape, his light gray pants and polished boots. Beneath his frock coat he wore a narrow belt from which a six-shot colt hung half concealed.

He finished the whiskey and, as he fixed his eyes on the table, he was tense when he saw that there were places for three.

"What does this mean? Do you have guests?

"Yes one; but do not worry. You will not think that I am trying to lay a trap for you.

"If I had thought so, I would not have come.

"In that case, I hope you are calm and don't commit any savagery. My house is a neutral ground in which everyone who enters is safe.

"What do you mean by that?

"That, even if I had summoned your worst enemy here, you could have the guarantee that nothing was going to happen.

"Do you want to explain yourself clearly, Agnes?

"I'll explain myself, because it's about ten o'clock and I don't want you to suffer a surprise that could unbalance your nerves. The missing guest is Foot.

Fritt stood up violently, but she, with a cold look, restrained him by saying:

"Do you want to be still? I have assured you that nothing is going to happen ... at least here. Now I will tell you another thing; I have summoned the two of you because I understand that it is time for you to speak up and settle your differences as amicably as possible. You are devouring each other for no use and that is stupid. I do not think that with good will it is difficult to reach an agreement.

Fritt wryly asked:

"Who has hinted at that, Foot?

"Do not. It was me. I told him the other night and he seemed to think about it a lot, but he replied that he couldn't come up with a solution on his own; instead, he agreed to discuss the matter with you. That is why I have allowed myself to meet the two of you for dinner. I hope that a good digestion makes you a bit optimistic.

"Well, I thank you for your good will; But do you realize what can happen if he knows I'm here while I didn't know he was coming?

"I realize everything, but with those misgivings it is not going anywhere. You will not believe me so stupid that I play my skin committing a betrayal that would not bring me any benefit. Neither you nor he can do anything because I have taken my precautions. One of you will leave here first, escorted by four men of mine who will not hesitate to use the revolver at the slightest hint of treachery, and the other will leave in the same way.

"After they have left you in your lairs, I will wash my hands of what may happen, although if you have a little common sense, you will leave here with a commitment that benefits both of you. I think that, instead of being suspicious, what you should do is think about an arrangement formula. It is more practical than all that.

Fritt fell silent and she gave herself to the task of finishing the table in order.

Shortly after, the black maid who served him opened the door to announce:

"Ma'am, Mr. Foot is out there.

"Tell him to pass.

Fritt stood up, arm stiff in case danger arose. Agnes, as if she hadn't seen him, stepped in front of him, facing the door.

Foot appeared tense and looked around. When he discovered his rival, he stood at the door waiting and Agnes, smiling, said:

Come in, Foot, and have no fear. We are among friends.

He came forward. "The Californian Beauty", extending her well-shaped arms one to each of the two gunmen, ordered:

"Your revolvers. As it is not the polite person to dine with weapons at hand, please give them to me. We will dine with more tranquility and there will be no fear that any of them will go off. When you leave I will return them to you.

Foot was the first to obey, and handed over the revolver. Fritt followed suit.

She locked them with a key in a drawer and, pointing to their place at the table, added:

"And now, to dinner without further worries. After dinner we will talk about what is convenient or not convenient to do, but at the very least, don't make my dinner bitter.

They both took their seats and the black woman began to serve the table. Until the end, Agnes was commenting on her own on the situation, the sterility of that fight between the two colossi, which well protected could not defeat each other, and, finally, how beneficial it would be for both of them to find a point of agreement to cease in the fight and be able to enjoy his hegemony with more tranquility and better income.

"As you will understand," he added, "I don't care about your rivalry, because I neither win nor lose with it. I am on the fringes of your struggles, because out of gallantry or whatever, I am in the middle of the street of San Francisco like an island surrounded by water on all sides. If I had seen myself stuck in the swell of that stormy sea in which you are agitated, you should have counted on me, because, although a woman, I have enough courage not to let myself be overwhelmed by anyone.

"For this very reason, and because I appreciate both of you, that is why I ask you to be sensible and practical. A bird in hand is better than a hundred flying, and if you have not yet wanted to realize a reality, I will tell you. The people of the gambling dens are getting tired of being besieged by one and the other.

Although reluctantly, they are willing to help you in a sensible way, as a lesser evil, but if you try to annihilate them twice, the day will come when you will have them in front of you and things will get too ugly for everyone. Therefore, I beg you to put pride aside and be practical. I believe that without humiliating each other it will not be difficult to come to an agreement.

None answered. The two were pondering their recommendations and looking for a formula that would benefit them without giving up in a humiliating way.

When coffee and rum were served after dessert, Agnes ordered the dishes to be lifted and, lighting a cigarette, after offering them cigars, she said:

"Well, what do you have to answer?

The two glared at each other. Fritt was the first to reply:

"I don't know, Agnes; I find it difficult.

"What about you, Foot?

"I dont know. All I can admit, and it is already concede, is that we divide the income equally.

Fritt chimed in:

"It's not as easy as it sounds, Foot, even if I accepted it. What is the income and who is going to collect it?

"We would draw lots," replied Foot.

"It doesn't suit me ... or you. We would distrust each other about loyalty in the cast and in the collection. There are always ways to cheat.

"Yes. A little dangerous, but you could prove it.

"I don't know ... I'm not convinced ... he's poor.

Agnes, who was looking at them mockingly, intervened:

"Well, I see that you are only good for pulling a revolver and shooting, but otherwise, you have very little worth under your hair. I am going to give you the solution and I think there is nothing better. If you do not accept it, you will prove to be two pumpkins.

»By a whim of chance, my joint is in the center of the city and in the center of this street. It is like a sword that cuts her in two. Well, the solution is that one of you will be the owner of half the city and the other owner of the other half. From here down, for one and from here up, for another. What you get from your fiefdoms is up to your organization, without the other intervening, and thus, not having to pay more than just one, the owners of premises will feel calmer, knowing that the adjusted will be the only thing they will have to disburse.

»So that there is no dispute, you will turn heads and tails to see who corresponds to one sector or another and once agreed, solemnly promise not to interfere where it does not correspond to you. Fights will be avoided, you will be able to alternate calmly between one and the other and the benefits will be net and without complications.

»If you don't like the solution, since you don't have a better solution, you can get up and get ready to leave. I have already done enough for your cause and I will leave each one of you in your homes. If after time you have completely undone, it will matter very little to me, because you have wanted it that way.

The two stared at each other. Actually, it was a good formula, in which the self-esteem of each one was not lowered.

Foot replied:

"Fritt has the floor.

"If you accept, I am willing to accept it.

"In that case, no more talk, Fritt. I think it has been the most viable solution. You represent one force and I another, since we have had the power to eliminate the competition by half, it is fair that we half enjoy the benefit.

Fritt filled their glasses and offered one to Agnes and one to Foot. He raised his and offered:

"By the ingenuity of Agnes, who is the most wonderful and cunning woman I have ever met.

"For her and for her posterity.

"For your reconciliation," Agnes said.

They put their glasses together and the crystals vibrated when they collided. Once the content was completed, Foot indicated:

"You flip the coin, Agnes. Let Fritt choose.

She took a gold coin out of her purse and held it up in the lamplight. Then he said:

"When it's in the air, ask. Face the south part and cross the north part.

"Cara," Fritt said.

The coin fell tails. She stated:

"The north for Foot and the south for you. Are you satisfied?

"Agree; do not talk more.

"So, to shake hands and be good friends. There is a lot of field to exploit and a lot of benefit for both. The arrangement will be talked about a lot, but people will accept it without reservation and your men will not have to kill each other on every corner like now.

The two men held out their rough hands and shook them tightly. It seemed that the pact was sincere and that both were satisfied with that solution, which gave them a great respite.

"Now," Agnes added, "let your men know. Where have you left them?

Foot stated:

"I have only brought with me Fred Prestley, my second. He'll be at the bar.

"I have also brought my second, Frank Wymen, and he will be walking down the street.

"So, let's go down to the bar together. I'll bring Frank in to join you and get the news.

He took them by the arm and going out onto the gallery descended into the living room. It was something that aroused the most lively curiosity to see "the Californian Beauty" with them by the arm, and, above all, to see the two gunmen together and smiling.

Fred didn't want to believe what he was seeing and rubbed his eyes. Foot stepped ahead of him, saying:

"Fred, shake hands with Fritt, we have signed peace in a beneficial agreement. From this moment, the city is divided into two sectors; from here up our completely, and from here down, from Fritt. You will let the boys know and warn them from me that whoever does not respect the agreement and overreaches will have to deal with me.

Fred reluctantly accepted the invitation and shook Fritt's hand. At that moment, the second of this one, appeared in the bar and showed the same strangeness.

Fritt explained the arrangement, and Frank seemed to welcome it more enthusiastically. He was tired of risking his life every day without a moment of calm that allowed him to enjoy his winnings with relative ease.

That night, the four alternated in the premises to celebrate the pact and at dawn they left, confirming their willingness to carry it out.

At the door they parted, each taking a different direction. When they were out of sight, Fred, who had his mental reservations, asked:

"Do you really think that toad will respect this?

"Yes I do, Fred. He, like me, is fed up with this fight without profit. There will come a time when we will not find men who want to join our side, no matter how well we pay them. You know the uneasiness of getting up without knowing if one will be able to lie down, always jumping to kill, with the revolver in hand and without guessing where death is going to come.

Now, at least, each of us will devote himself to plundering his part, and in it we will be the masters. By not alternating in the opposite and not getting into what the rival does, crashes will be avoided. If you fight for something, it will be among yourselves, and so we can organize the collection of our benefits more harshly.

"That's fine, as long as someone doesn't lose their temper and get out of position. I think the worst part has come to him, because in the south there are better places that can pay a higher fee. He should have chosen the south.

"We raffled it, which was the logical thing to do.

"Well, now, whose job is it to get the juice out of" Californian Beauty "?

"To nobody. That is neutral ground.

"Why that concession? Agnes earns a lot and had to pay. It is something we lose.

"You don't lose anything. Somewhere the division had to begin. If it had been Fritt's turn, it would be for him. Also, thanks to her, it has come to this. Leave Agnes alone.

Fred didn't say anything, but chewed on his thin mustache. He hated Agnes, because he had conceited certain concessions from her that even his own boss could never get. This contempt of a woman for a man of courage like him, and also of good shape, did not satisfy him. She had gotten unimpeded favors from others much younger than her, and she didn't accept failure.

But knowing that Foot felt for Agnes a strange and sentimental weakness that put her under his protection, he did not dare to strengthen his protests.

Anyway, it would be something he wouldn't leave dead. He was stubborn as a good Texan and he harbored his plans for the future, projects that perhaps that pact had delayed, since he always hoped that, if Foot fell in the fight, he could be named his replacement, because he was the toughest , cruel and daring of the gang.

To some extent, he was glad that the unalterable fiefdom of "Californian Beauty" had not belonged to anyone. It was a neutral place to be able to visit without misgivings, and since he hadn't been able to get anything from Agnes, there was something there that was also interesting to him; It was Betty, "La Rubia", the main attraction of the place; a girl of about twenty, graceful, pretty and attractive, who stood out above all the cast.

He liked her extraordinarily and although he did not seem to pay much attention to her wooing, he intended to besiege her until he had overcome her resistance. Two failures in a row in the same place, it wasn't something he was willing to fit in.

Now, free of enemies and worries, he would dedicate himself to tightening the siege more vigorously, and if "the Blonde" resisted him, he would show her how he knew how to handle prim and hostile women.

CHAPTER III

A THIRD IN DISCORD

The ideal goal for all adventurers in the American West, but not for the soft and timid adventurers who dream of making their fortune in a smooth and measured way, was San Francisco. They had nothing to do on the wild coast, if it was not to withdraw from the path of the daring, and in this sense they could gather little from the poor crumbs that they were left as despicable.

The man who ventured into the city of the hills knew, no matter how little knowledge he had of the prevailing climate there, that he was exposing himself to much if he wanted to profit from his attack, and thus, those who entered the dusty street every day. of San Francisco were not unaware that their life was only worth what chance would like to value for it, because in every corner, in every gambling den door, in every poker or roulette table, death mounted the guard anxious to get its part in the zarabanda of selfishness and overflowing passions.

Nobody feared the law, where the law was a myth. Each one wore his at the waist and everything depended on how he knew how to apply it and how quickly he used to be victorious.

Men like Foot and Fritt were almost common in the city, as were many others, whose names needed too much space to list. During the time that the gold empire lasted in the Pearl of the Pacific, they were renewed with unusual frequency, because death was in charge of accelerating the clearing of their ranks to make way for those who were pouring in, happy to be able to cover their ranks.

Perhaps the only decent note that could be found was that robberies, fights and deaths took place, with few exceptions, among that mob. It was a nest of snakes that devoured each other, and they did not do it out of kindness, but because for their vanity as thugs and rough men it was not a halo to kill a wretch without courage or courage to face them. "To kill their man," as they said in the tragic slang of the city, was to suppress another as brave, swift, and daring as they. This was indeed a poster to display as a trophy to impose respect on those who, showing off as thugs, could show their faces.

After a month of the pact tacitly agreed between Foot and Fritt, a period of relative calm seemed to reign in San Francisco. This did not mean that there were no brawls and that the colts did not bark sinisterly at night, but it all boiled down to isolated squabbles, chance encounters, or disputes caused by excess alcohol or interest derived from the gaming tables.

The members of the two gangs, respecting superior orders, had limited themselves to developing their activities in the areas assigned to each. It was tried to fix the mess of taxes to the locals to avoid the rebellions and everything seemed to go as smoothly.

Fred, Foot's second, had taken advantage of the truce to visit Agnes's joint more regularly. Freer from work and without the need to take extreme precautions to defend his life, he gave himself up to an existence of fun and ease that up to that moment had been forbidden to him.

And his most determined endeavor was to render the sullen and accentuated contempt of Betty, "the Blonde." His vanity as a capricious man, spoiled by almost all the wretches who consumed their poor lives in the gambling dens, did not agree with that contemptuous treatment, and using a stickiness that made the girl curl, he besieged him in all shades, even to insinuate threats of violence if he did not agree to their claims.

So stubborn was he that the young woman went to Agnes. He knew the preponderance that this one had acquired with the two roosters of the town and hoped that a pressure of her on Foot would force his second to desist and to be more restrained.

Agnes listened kindly to her and replied:

"If you don't like Fred, I shouldn't advise you. I have been very free to choose my loves in life and I have not given in to threats either. If you don't want to be convinced that you're wasting your time, I'll see to it that you understand.

Until one night, Agnes was forced to intervene on behalf of the girl. She was a valuable asset to her joint, and she was self-conscious and nervous when Fred was in the living room and she had to work.

And as this harmed his interests because the girl did not serve the clientele with the necessary pleasure and dynamism, he lost patience and addressing the gunman, he squared off before him, saying:

Listen, Fred; Your being my friend Foot's henchman doesn't give you the right to meddle in the affairs of my establishment. I've given you time to convince yourself that Betty doesn't want anything with you and it's about time it entered your head. You make her nervous, you make me and you harm both of us in our interests. Convince yourself that you have nothing to do there and go to hell at once, but don't get over my head.

Fred could not admit that a woman would treat him with such humiliating harshness and he stirred in anger, answering:

"Don't give yourself too much importance, Agnes. You are believing yourself to be the queen of San Francisco because Foot is too stupid allowing himself to be dominated by you, and if you think that I am like him, you are wrong. Bite your tongue and don't threaten me, because they will weigh you down.

She, undeterred, looked him straight ahead and replied:

"You are the idiot and you don't realize it. Neither with the friendship of your boss nor without it, I consent to anyone who tries to impose on me in my house, and don't look at me like that, because you have a dozen revolvers pointing at you and at a signal from me they will shoot you right there. Betty wants nothing more than to lose sight of you, and if you want to keep frequenting my house, you'd do well to leave her alone. Don't make me ask Foot to forbid you to come in here anymore. I would not like to make you that humiliation, but if you force me, I will not hesitate, because I am more than a vulgar woman, even if you believe otherwise. If men like Foot and Fritt have given me importance, you have too little to take it from me.

Fred was purple at the contemptuous reprimand thrown out loud in front of the clientele. He had a wild desire to draw his revolver and silence that sharp tongue that was wounding him like a knife, but he did not disdain the warning. Eight tough, tense men at a safe distance formed a menacing semicircle, and he knew that no matter how swift he was handling the colt, he would only get himself killed, even if he took the hideous woman away.

Biting her lips in anger, she bellowed:

"I am very free to woo whoever I want, since it is nothing of yours.

"It will be outside my establishment, but inside, no. You annoy me and you harm me and I have a business to exploit it and not to provide you with fun. Find out about this and do not force me to take any steps against you.

Exasperated, the gunman replied:

"I warn you that Foot is not the bogeyman, at least for me, he serves me and I serve him and he can only get involved in the things of our business. Outside of them, I am free to do what I want and what I want. If it seems good to you like that, delighted, and if not ... it will be as I want.

"Don't brag so much, Fred. Your boss won't let you do your whim because you want to. Don't be a fool.

"Neither he nor anyone else will stop me from doing it, if it's my whim. Where one man can put another, and if I have been by his side until now, it will not have been a coward.

"That matters little to me, Fred; but don't pull too much on the rope. You are used to doing many things and you think that they are all easy. I am a very tough nut to crack.

"You are vain. Adventurers like you have come here in droves and lasted as long as we wanted them to last.

"Until I arrived, and some idiotic men like you, they lasted less. When you come here on another plan, I will be happy to receive you and even to forget your rudeness. I cannot ask you to behave like a senator, because there are certain things that can only be achieved by being born twice, but I will demand that you leave everything around me alone. Please go ... at least for tonight. Maybe the fresh air will calm you down a bit and make you see things from another point of view.

And if I didn't want to leave, what would happen?

"Don't ask me, Fred. It would be embarrassing for you if I told you, and I believe you with common sense to know me. I beg you to go, and that's enough.

He understood what she meant. Those eight guys who didn't lose sight of him would force him out one way or another. It was better to do it of your own free will and not lead to something that would not have an easy solution.

And getting up angrily from the table, he threw a handful of dollars on the board and left the premises.

For several days he was without going to the gambling den. Agnes realized this and judged that the threat had been strong enough to command respect for the gunman. The strength of his boss was not debatable without betrayal and he had many people who would defend him if it exploded by any of his components, even if it was Fred.

Therefore, he did not bother to report the incident to Foot with his second. He was afraid it would lead to a bitter argument between them and he wanted to avoid it wisely.

But a week later, Fred, who had been drinking more than necessary in other bars in conjunction with his companions, felt the attraction that Betty continued to exert on him and forgetting his argument with Agnes and disdaining at the time what might happen, he decided return to the gambling den of «La Bella Californiana».

But this time his presence was more dangerous. Alcohol encouraged him excessively and Fred was a man who, when drunk, lacked all control.

And so, with his eyes on fire and the desire to fight in his blood, he appeared in the room when it was more animated and when its owner expected less an incident that would disturb the peace that for some days had reigned in his establishment.

* * *

Chance has quirks that are sometimes comic and sometimes dramatic. This time, in tune with the atmosphere of the city, he had a rather hard whim and this one had a name: Stuart Sterling.

Stuart was the one hundred percent type of adventurer, for whom the world was such an insignificant space that its dimensions were too narrow for him.

In his twenty-eight years of exuberant and hectic life, he had traveled thousands of miles pulsing environments, studying customs, drawing lessons and getting bored without being able to avoid it, because the emotions suffered in all that long exodus could not fulfill the measure of his desires and he continued looking for the climate heated to the impossible that would leave him satisfied at once to retire to a peaceful life after parodying the phrase "I arrived, saw and conquered."

He had flown barges on the Mississippi, fought savagely in port coffeehouses and taverns, chased bison along the Ohio, drove stagecoaches on the eastern routes, fought with the Indians on the central plains driving caravans on the Santa Fe route, officiated As a good man (and to say good meant strong to impose calm) in the worst gambling dens of San Antonio and Austin, he extracted salt from the Humboldt mines and gold from those of Virginia City, and when he reached the rough San Francisco, and the favorable climate for making money in it, he stuffed the gold dust that was his entire fortune into a canvas sack, reviewed his double set of revolvers with some fanciful notches in their blackened butts, and took the course of the wild coast ready to be noticed in it,for his greatest vanity was not to go unnoticed anywhere.

At heart, Stuart was a naive man, hardened by life, with a spirit that had a mixture of good and evil, which depending on the way the precipitate was stirred, exploded one way or another.

Along with rock-hard actions, he had bizarre bouts of romanticism. Once he had fought fiercely with ten Indians who surrounded him. In strength of courage, marksmanship and skill, he managed to shoot down six and then charged the remaining four, wounding and pulling their hair while they were still breathing, an action that put him on the same level as the Redskins. However, among the wounded there was a boy of about fourteen, who, although he had fought with him fiercely, accused he was still a child.

Unconcerned, he healed him as best he could, carried him on his back and, exposing himself to being shot with arrows by his tribe, took him to the tribe and left him near the "teepees", returning to his starting point. Hundreds of these traits could be counted, and for this reason it was very difficult to classify him in a general section between good and bad.

When he arrived in San Francisco one sunny and joyful morning, he was ecstatic contemplating the waste of gold that the star king poured over the splendid bay, and he told himself at the prospect that it was worth living there, even if it was a short stage.

He was so absorbed by the contemplation of the sea that he stood tense at the breakwater with the bulging luggage on land beside him and his bright pupils fixed on that wonderful painting.

This prevented him from realizing in time something fundamental to him. One of the many undesirable failures that swarmed the city, discovered him, and seeing him alone, well dressed and with that promising luggage, did not hesitate to give him a rather unpleasant reception. He approached him cautiously from behind and applying the barrel of his revolver to his waist, he ordered:

"Keep looking at the sea at your leisure and don't move. I will lighten your weight so that you can walk more at ease later.

Stuart didn't bother to turn his head. With perfect calm, he replied:

"Well friend, that's called getting up early to welcome me. What interests you about me?

"All that is worth it.

"Oh! The best thing about my person is me. Are you interested?

"Absolutely. Nothing but the money, the luggage and the revolver.

"You are wrong to disdain my worth, friend. If they were to charge me stripped of all that they ask of me, it would be worth much more than what they intend to take. You will find my money in my wallet, here around my waist I have a sack tied with a few pounds of gold dust, my colt is here. Take it however you think is most comfortable and safe for you.

The undesirable tried to snatch the revolver from his back and reached out to remove the weapon. At that moment, Stuart, dropping to the ground, tugged at the arm and dragged the robber away. He turned, falling sideways and although he fired, the shot did not hit a target.

There the incident ended. With a powerful punch to the chin, he knocked him out, and then, taking him as if he were a feather, he lifted him into the void, advanced with him, and threw him effortlessly off the breakwater into the sea.

For a moment he curiously followed the circles formed by the water at the place of the fall, widening until it broke in the surf, and when he was convinced that it would no longer come out, he murmured:

"Poor devil, he was definitely not born to be a robber!

And with this funeral oration, he took up his sack again and went to the village.

After looking for accommodation, which was neither easy nor cheap, he decided to orient himself and for two nights he frequented some gambling dens. From the conversations he was able to capture, he drew a conclusion: that infernal paradise had two owners and these owners were named Foot and Fritt, who, by force of daring, lived majestically at the expense of the effort of others.

That system of exploiting gambling den owners demanding an amount to guarantee their establishments seemed like a discovery. After all, it was something quite vulgar, that with a few men of heart could be achieved, and after weighing the wide field that the town offered, it was said that there was room not only for two, but for three. Everything consisted of rectifying borders and better dividing the field of operations.

The business, he thought, was not very honest, but demanding a part of its profits that were not very clear to certain exploiters could not be described as a great sin. If vice yielded a lot for certain exploiters to live, making room for one more didn't mean much. A little less for others and a little for himself.

He presumed that they would not give it to him willingly and that he would have to fight with some opposition, but when you were bold, tough and brave like him you could try to take part in the game. Whoever was not satisfied, who tried to oppose it if he could.

I was curious to meet the two leaders of the operating bands. Perhaps he could reach an amicable arrangement with them, and even join their organization with a good percentage. He was good for many things and they wouldn't give him anything for free, but if they refused, he would take it on his own as he could.

When he inquired about how to get in touch with either of them, he learned that his idea was not as easy as he thought. Both lived in mystery and well guarded, but they used to frequent the joint of "La Bella Californiana" and perhaps there he would have the opportunity to meet one of the two.

And he devoted himself to frequenting the establishment in the hope of an incidental encounter with someone; more had been a few days that they did not appear at the premises and he was forced to let time pass without luck accompanying him in his wishes. Stuart, a happy, dynamic man with a great desire to enjoy life, decided to make the best of that time, and as he was handsome, attractive, funny in his witty and well dancing, he gave himself up to the task of entertaining his evenings with the girls from the cast of Agnes, his will and sympathies quickly being captured, since he was not rude in his dealings and knew how to be with them as gallant as he was rude.

But among all the girls, Betty had a particular attraction for him. He found her more elegant, more refined, more attractive and more seductive, and he made her the object of his preferences, without thereby disturbing her in her obligations within the establishment.

Agnes did not fail to notice the boisterous presence of the stranger and his assiduousness towards Betty, but since he was polite and restrained, she had nothing to oppose that preference. He believed her to be the flower of a few nights, and as long as he spent his gold lavishly and did not demoralize his girls, he not only tolerated him, but began to find him sympathetic and agreeable.

This made her forget about Fred. The fact that he hadn't returned to the establishment seemed like a good sign. He must have realized the damage that could cause him to insist on his claims, and apparently he had given up on the girl to fix his cloudy eyes on someone else from a different gambling den.

Until nights later, when she least expected it, she saw him come in frowning, his eyes too bright and a crude gesture of defiance that she didn't like.

And he was on guard. If, despite already feeling, he joined the jealousy that the stranger's deferences for Betty could ignite in him, something serious was going to happen that would change the face of things from now on or cause a sudden and bloody explosion.

CHAPTER IV

STUART BEGINS THE GAME

Fred hesitantly entered the den, and after wandering his cloudy gaze around, smiled cruelly, taking a seat at a small table that happened to be unoccupied. He ordered whiskey in a hoarse voice and when it was served he clutched the glass with a nervous pulse and drank some of the contents, wiping his dry lips with the back of his hand. Then he was tense, examining everyone in the room.

The girls danced on the tabladillo to the beat of lively and frisky music that the upright piano played a bit bitterly. They danced a noisy cancan, and almost all the customers were absorbed in the contemplation of the suggestive swaying of the girls.

Stuart, who sat at a table next to the table, smiled cheerful and dynamic, winking at Betty, who from time to time gave him an expressive look or gave him a picaresque wink that broadened the smile on the adventurer's face even more. .

Fred, although drunk, did not stop picking up those signs of intelligence and felt an aggressive curiosity to know to whom they were addressed, but there were so many customers crowded around the tables near the stage that it was not easy for him to locate the favored one.

But instinct told him that there was someone more fortunate than he, who had managed to grasp the girl's sympathy, and his teeth gritted furiously. He was there ready to make a fuss, and Betty's gestures would serve as a pretext to make a fuss.

Agnes, who alternated with two rich cattlemen in a strategic place from which she observed the whole room, noticed Fred's somewhat aggressive presence, and fearing that something tragic might happen she tried to avoid it.

For this, when the dance ended and before the girls left the room, he got up, crossed between the tables and approaching the one that Stuart was occupying, he said in a low voice:

Listen, stranger. You are a very nice man and a good customer, but at this moment you are a powder keg with the fuse burning and I would like to put it out.

"Devil! "Exclaimed Stuart surprised." What have I done to qualify me like this?

"Nothing yet, but he can do it. At this moment there is someone in the living room who has come wanting to disturb the tranquility that reigns here. You will not know him, but if you have heard of Konny Foot, you will realize what this name means.

"Konny Foot? I have heard of him and I am eager to meet him. Tell me who it is.

"Oh, it's not about him! If it were Foot, I would be calm, because he is a great friend of mine. It's about Fred Prestley, his second, a too harsh guy, who is infatuated with Betty, and since she has scorned him, he feels angry to the point of aggression.

"I had to seriously threaten to complain to his boss and I kicked him out of here a few days ago. I thought he had resigned himself, but I see that he has not, because he has just appeared and not in very good condition. He must have had too much to drink, and I suspect he is in the mood to make a fuss.

"A nice view that I don't want to miss, ma'am," Stuart replied cheerfully. It is something that tempers my nerves and you have done well to warn me, because that way I will not miss even the slightest detail.

"Yes but no. You will only start to put it together if you notice that Betty makes a face to you and you to her. It is better that you leave the girl alone tonight to avoid any fuss. Fred is so wild, that I would put myself in a compromise, not only because of what the order affects, but because of his boss and I want to avoid it.

"Why don't you go to him, lift his jacket off, and spank him for being unruly? I consider her capable of doing it, but ... well, I think it's advice that I shouldn't give a woman. You better tell me who that puppet is. I wouldn't like to be caught off guard.

"Well look at the door and the third table on the left will tell you who it is. He is alone in it.

"Thanks. I will look at him and keep an eye on him, but now answer a question: why have you hired this precious girls choir here?

"So that they brighten up the premises and serve as an incentive to customers.

"Just. And so that they dance with them, and alternate, and force to spend, is not that?

"I cannot deny that they charge for that.

"That being the case, why would he admit that a guy from outside the house wants to impose himself against his customs? It surprises me that a woman of his quality can tolerate it.

"I do not tolerate it, but faced with the possibility of something serious happening, I prefer to compromise.

"Which is as much as letting yourself be humiliated by someone who feels that whim. Well, if you think so, I don't. I am not a man capable of withstanding the impositions of anyone nor am I afraid of anyone, no matter how bully they feel. You should do the same, because with that procedure, if he wanted to, every night this room would become a missionary's compound, where we should all be quiet to hear him brag.

»The worst thing that can be done is to give wings to those who do not know how to use them. For my part, I will tell her, feeling very sorry, that I will dance with Betty if she does not refuse of her own free will, and if I see that she refuses because she is afraid of that guy, I will ask her to dance whether she wants it or not, because I would consider him a contempt to make me that ugly for no reason in front of everyone. I have nothing to do with the girl, nor do I try to impose myself on her, but here she comes to fulfill a mission and I pay for that mission to enjoy her. Neither Fred, nor his boss, nor his entire crew, would stop me from doing whatever I wanted without forcing anyone.

Agnes looked at him between admiration and annoyance and replied:

"Do you realize what that can mean?

"Exactly the same as it can be for him.

"And what does it mean for me?

"You are not going to tell me that you are a fearful woman, or that this guy is going to eat you. When you live in San Francisco and a place like this is exploited without the help of any man, it is because you have the nerve and courage to face all the setbacks that arise. I don't think that Fred is more than many others who have come here wanting to fight.

"By itself it isn't, but your boss ...

"To hell with your boss! If, as you claim, he is your friend, he will prove it to you. On the other hand, I am the one who is going to show my face and not you. Leave me alone and walk away. If that guy comes to teach him about things he does not know, I will take care of being his teacher and you will never be responsible for what may happen between him and me.

Agnes looked at him in admiration as she observed the steadiness and calm of this cold stranger. After a moment of hesitation, he replied:

"You seem very sure of yourself.

"As sure as one day I will own San Francisco. It's something that has gotten into my head and I'll get it. As this is not achieved by bending the spine before the people, but by making it bend, I am prepared for everything.

"Very ambitious, stranger. Forget that those who are the masters here today have had to fight a lot and dangerously to be so.

"Well, we will fight like them or better. Go away and leave me, because there I see Betty and this matter is mine and nobody else's.

And getting up calmly, he left the table to go out to meet the girl.

Agnes was left tense for a moment not knowing what decision to make, but Stuart's courage and self-confidence had won her over. He guessed that if Fred tried something dangerous he was going to fail miserably and shrugged. The way the gunman was setting things up, this had to come someday and it was almost preferable for a stranger to do it, sparing her the responsibility of forcing her men to intervene directly in the matter.

He retired back to his table without losing sight of Fred, while Stuart walked calmly to meet Betty.

The piano was already reeling off its melodies, inviting customers to dance and Stuart tried to link the young woman in the waist, but Betty had already discovered Fred catching the threatening looks he was throwing him. Therefore, ignoring that his partner was imposed on the tense situation, he pleaded:

"Would you like to let me rest for a while? I am fatigued from work and would appreciate it if ...

"Wait a minute," Stuart cut off "; no excuses, because I am on the street of what is happening. I think if you start to show any guy that you are afraid of him, you will be lost, and I, for my part, am not prepared to make a fool of myself. We will dance and ... fear not. If that guy's nerves get triggered, something worse will shoot me first. Come on, girl.

And before she had time to reject him, he squeezed her around the waist and pulled her onto the floor.

Betty resigned herself. Someday the explosive had to go off, and if she delayed it, perhaps then she would not have a man as whole and determined as that to protect her properly.

When Fred observed that the young woman danced with Stuart, he felt a strange vibration in his entire being, and he threw withering glances at the girl, in which he held a terrible threat to her if she continued dancing, but the adventurer held her tightly around the waist and for nothing in the world would he have allowed her to get rid of him.

Furthermore, to better control Fred's movements, he dragged Betty to that side. He did not want the other couples to obstruct his vision by hiding any movement of the gunman.

Thus it was approaching dangerously towards him; Betty was almost on the verge of fainting, as she guessed the tragic end of that scene in which the nerves of the hateful gallant must be red hot.

And actually, they were. The jilted gunman, livid as paper, clenched his teeth, interlocking them as if trying to fuse them together. Without knowing why, he understood that this unknown guy was exceeding in igniting his anger, as if he knew the truth of his feelings, and his vanity as a humiliated man would not agree to go through such a situation.

Suddenly he jumped out of the seat like a rabid cat and planted himself in front of the couple. Stuart, who did not lose sight of him, abruptly released Betty, hiding her with his body, and with icy calm asked:

"Are you so bad on your nerves that you make those grotesque little jumps? Why are they not cared for? You scared us, friend.

But Fred, trying to grab the young woman by the arm, which Stuart hindered, launched a rude threat:

"I have told you that you do not dance anything except with me while I am here, and if I see you again in the arms of another man I will kill you like a dog.

Stuart looked at him coldly, asking:

"With whose permission?

"Without permission from anyone, because I don't usually ask for it, but rather to take it.

"And haven't you counted on me a bit?

"With you? Yes I think so.

His hand flicked to the revolver, tugging at it. Betty let out an amazing scream, putting her hands to her eyes in terror, and in response to the scream there was a detonation. Fred, with the revolver clutching the handle but no time to grasp the trigger, roared with fierce pain and desperately dropped the weapon to put his hands to his belly.

He squeezed it with savage fury, unable to prevent the blood from flowing through his convulsive fingers, and after drawing a tragic arc with his body, he fell facedown to the ground writhing in death throes of agony.

An impressive silence ensued in the living room. Then a cry of surprise broke out, and those closest to him surrounded the fallen man, eagerly examining him as if they were having a hard time convincing themselves that it had been possible to finish off this tough and seemingly invincible fellow after allowing him to draw.

The girls screamed hysterically. The pianist, faithful to his slogan, was pounding on the piano trying to impose himself on the tumult, and Agnes, advancing a little pale but serene, approached Stuart, commenting:

"What I feared... only the other way around.

"That is well commented", replied the adventurer smiling. I hope this incident ends here.

"I'm afraid it starts here, stranger. Now we need to know what Foot will think of the death of his second.

"I don't think it's going to eat me. I've allowed him to get the gun out before I did, and if he proved to be heavier handheld, it's not my fault.

"Okay, but that doesn't say anything. I'm afraid Foot doesn't see it kindly.

"It will be because they will not be as beautiful as I am. What is he afraid of, that he will be enraged because there is someone as fast as him with a gun in his hand? I don't think I'm trying to get the privilege of speed. You will have to admit it that way, and if you are not satisfied we can discuss the matter in the same way. I am a man who gives all possible facilities to resolve matters.

Agnes didn't answer. He was fearing that he was indeed too tough and dangerous a man and that Foot would regard him as a danger to her future safety.

Fred died almost suddenly with his intestines crossed and "the Californian Beauty", trying to control his nerves, commented:

"Be what the devil wants. Jim, take that man around in there; that they clean that blood and each one to his place. Betty, go to my rooms and compose yourself. You are as pale as the dead and thus you cannot act. John, go find Foot, and if you find him tell him for me to please come over here, because I urgently need to speak to him. As for you, "he added, addressing Stuart," I think the best thing you can do is to disappear from here, and if you do so from San Francisco, all the better. I will try to settle this matter with Foot.

"Thank you very much Agnes; You are a wonderful woman because you are strong and whole, one of those women that I like because there are very few, but I will also discuss this matter with Foot's coconut. I really wanted to meet him and a better time than this, none.

"You will say worst occasion. He will not be able to forgive her for killing the best of his men.

"And that was the best? What will the others be like! Much better am I, as I have shown, and if you need a replacement we can understand each other. I think it will suit him, because if he rejects me ... then I will supplant him one day. It is a decided thing and no one will make me back down from my idea.

"Do you think it will scare you?

"I guess not, but neither does he to me. It will be something that we can discuss in two ways. At your choice I let you choose what you like the most.

And calmly he went to sit down at the table again, filling his glass with a calm pulse, while Agnes, marveling at his cold blood, looked at him askance.

She, too, was beginning to like this guy who didn't look like any of those she'd ever met.

CHAPTER V

A BOLD PROPOSITION

Once order was restored, although with a certain nervousness, the customers returned to their tables, where the event was discussed passionately. This was something unusual and everyone wondered how the drama that had just begun, but which demanded a continuation difficult to predict, was going to end.

When Agnes was convinced that calm was reigning again, she called the chief of the men in her service to prevail over any tumult and said:

"Keep an eye out, although I don't expect anything out of the ordinary to happen. If Foot comes, hold him for a moment and send me a warning. I go to my rooms.

He approached Stuart, who had lit a cigarette, and begged him:

"Would you like to go up to my private rooms for a moment?

"Devil! Why not? That honors me exceedingly, because the sanctuary of a woman like you must be a wonderful thing. I hope this is not cause for another fight.

She looked at him in a special way when she heard him. She remembered Foot's assiduity and loving pretensions and ended up smiling with amusement.

"I hope not, at least for tonight.

"Good thing, if they let me rest. Why do you say that?

"Because the matter is too serious for Foot to think of something unrelated to the death of his second.

"Thunder and lightning! It means that he too …

"I don't want to say anything, stranger. Those matters are left to me. Follow me

"Well, I don't want to get into his private life. If that vulture is in love with you, I will tell you that you are not as bad in taste as I had assumed.

"Thanks. You are too gallant.

"Do not. I am just nothing more. You belong to the type of women that I would have liked.

"What would they have? Don't you like any of them?

"Relatively. My taste is varied, but heart complications seem premature to me. Perhaps one day, when I have a throne of dollars or bags of gold, the time seems to have come to think about it.

"Too much time you give to time. It can grow old sooner.

"Well, in the meantime, I like some… uncomplicated.

"Betty for example?

"Betty… and some of the various other girls you have here. She proves to be a woman of taste by choosing them and I am a very broad man in my expenses when the thing deserves it … superficially.

"I do not.

"You are not going to tell me that you have not liked a man in your life.

"Yes. Many, but … for various reasons, also superficial. Instead, for the only thing that I would totally like a man … I haven't found him yet.

"If it is worth a tip, do not delay in looking for it or you will be left without it. Being too demanding can expose her to not finding you in time.

"Do you think it is already too late for me?

"Do not. Not that, but don't let it be.

"Thanks. I'll study the advice when I have time.

They had reached the gallery. She, guiding him ahead, led him to his rooms, but left him in the reception room to take a look at Betty, who had fallen on her bed in a frenzy.

The young woman seemed asleep and tiptoeing out of the bedroom returned to Stuart's side.

He was pouring whiskey and had lit a cigar that he sucked with delight.

Agnes, smiling, commented:

"I note that you are not very much looked at to satisfy their tastes.

"I was ahead of your invitation, that's all. I was sure he would offer me whiskey and cigars; It is always the obligatory thing to do with trust visits, isn't it?

"You are very smart. What else do you think I can offer you?

"Don't make a vain man judge me.

"You do well not to be, because maybe you were wrong", she replied, smiling mischievously.

"It would be a shame, but since I don't like to fail in my convictions, it is preferable that he not tell me.

"I can offer you my protection, which is not small.

"I don't doubt it, but what concept can a man offer him who relies on a woman to succeed?

"A lousy opinion, but you have not understood me. It is not a protection to climb without merit, but to find the free way for that climb. If you were not useful to get there, the aid would be of no use.

"Maybe it would be something useful. As I would do it?

"Using my great friendship with Foot. Perhaps I could persuade him to accept his services in replacement of Fred.

"What interest do you have in Foot?

"He is my friend.

"Just your friend?

"It is just what I want it to be.

"Leave him as he is in that case, because I would not like to leave her wrong with him and cause a conflict. Perhaps one day my ambition will lead me to want to occupy that position and I would feel self-conscious about your recommendation. I prefer that he chooses freely and what may explode afterwards is a matter of both of us.

"Don't be stupid or vain. There were many gutsy men here before you who persisted in just that and now rest quietly and meditate on their follies a few inches underground.

"If he could kill his competitors, why couldn't I kill him if he wanted to? There is no invulnerable man, and what one does can be done by another.

"Maybe, but I don't want that to happen. Be satisfied if he thinks you are useful. The second place next to Foot is very category.

"And to replace Foot much more. Would you have settled for being in a joint like this something similar to what Betty is here?

"I have been and I settled until my time came, but not in your way. Women succeed with skill and without blood. You do it with gunshots.

"Each one uses whatever weapons he can. At the end of the day, believe it or not, yours are more dangerous.

"Don't be stubborn. Listen to me, why don't you just give that up and accept something else?

"The fact that?

"The position of my trusted man in the gambling den. I would pay you well and I would like to have a man as whole as you by my side.

"I reject it. I am very dangerous when I spend some time next to a woman. I would end up falling in love with you and I don't want to.

He said it in a jovial tone and Agnes looked at him intensely to ask:

"Do I seem so ugly or old that I scare you?"

"If it were so, I would accept it, because I would not be in danger of falling in love with you. You are attractive and I think you are too dangerous a woman. I don't like fighting with women and you and I would fight over one thing.

"Why?

"Because of any other woman.

"Because of Betty? Tonight you have fought not with her, but for her.

"Do not. It has not been precisely because of her, although it has served as a pretext. I would have killed myself with Fred for any trifle to see benefit in it, but this does not mean that I am not happy that she has benefited.

"You are an absurd man and I don't quite understand you," Agnes assured, annoyed by the clarity of Stuart's words.

He replied:

"But I'm honest, which is the main thing. I have had many ambitions in my life and I have fought to see them fulfilled. Later, they seemed poor and petty to me, perhaps because they were already achieved, not deserving more efforts, I abandoned them for new ones. I came to San Francisco because they told me it was the most wonderful city for my nerves and for making money. I have convinced myself that with gold you get everything in the world and I own very little, because until now I have not appreciated it.

»I want to earn money, but quickly, so as not to have time to take it with one hand and spend it with the other. The day I see myself with thousands and thousands of dollars at the same time, maybe I will appreciate what they are worth and feel like a saver, and that's why I'm going to try. If what happens to me, with everything, maybe when I get it I'll throw it away and suffer the last and most definitive disappointment of my life.

"Does the same thing happen to you with women?

"The same, at least up to the present. I fought to get some and then I was disappointed. Maybe it was because I didn't understand them ... or because they didn't understand me.

"You are absurd, not to call you something else.

"Call me whatever you want. It would not be the first and perhaps not the last.

"I believe it, but despite that, I predict one thing. The day a woman proposes it to you ... that day, you, with all that arsenal of contempt and unrealities, will be the most servile type when it comes to love. Ask whoever you can do so that she is not cruel and despotic, because if she is, she will make you pay once and for all what you could before do with the others.

"I don't believe in occasional fortune tellers, Agnes. I'm already too battered to pay for hazing.

"We all pay for them. Me too, and yet I wouldn't dare say that I can't afford them one day. There are times when, like worn screws, we go over the threading and ... we can no longer tighten as we would like.

"By then I will have died of old age, if not that I fell with my boots on.

One of the employees knocked on the door to announce that Foot was in the room. Agnes gave the order to be brought up.

Before the gunman arrived, he said to Stuart:

Think about it. It's up to me to convince Foot to ...

"Do not do it. I'm going to convince him by myself.

"I'm curious to see how you do it, but if you fail, don't expect me to intervene at the last minute. That is what is at stake.

"I will fight with what comes.

Foot knocked on the door and Agnes invited him inside. When the gunman discovered Stuart sitting comfortably in the armchair smoking his cigar with the glass of whiskey in front of him, he scowled at him and asked:

"A new guest?

"Not really, Foot. But circumstances have forced me to confine you here. I have something serious to report to you and this man is no stranger to it. You may not know him.

"Do not. I have never seen him.

Stuart got up saying:

"My name is Stuart Sterling. I think that for the moment the rest is striking.

"My name is Konny Foot. I suppose you will have some information about me that avoids adding more details.

"I have quite a lot of information, friend, and I am not deceiving you when I tell you that I had a great interest in meeting you. I wanted to talk to you and fate has done what it wants to make it happen. Agnes will inform you as she thinks best.

She invited Foot to sit down, and then she said:

"As I think I must start at the beginning, before you realize why, listen.

He recounted roughly the incidents that Fred had caused the previous days, the bitter argument they had the day he kicked him out of the joint, and how he had threatened the irascible Fred to tell his boss everything.

"Why haven't you done it before, Agnes? Foot interrupted. I would have forced him to ...

"I didn't think it was necessary," Agnes replied, "because he stopped visiting my establishment, but tonight he turned up drunk and in the mood for a fight. Taking advantage of the fact that he had finished the dance on the tabladillo, this client asked Betty to dance, and Fred, mad as a cat, thirsty, threatened to kill her if he saw her dancing with someone again.

You are a man and you would not allow a woman to disengage from your arms because of the threat of another man. That's what Stuart did; not spoil it and ask Fred if he had counted on him for the case. Fred's reply was to shoot the revolver, but the alcohol must have put lead in his hands, because he was too slow to fire. When he wanted to try, he had an ounce of lead in his belly. You have his corpse down in a room.

Foot jumped like a spring, roaring:

"What do you say? What ... has ... killed Fred? What killed him by letting him draw the gun?

"Below you have a hundred witnesses to the duel. You can go ask them.

Foot was stunned. He knew his second well enough to consider him one of the fastest and safest men with a colt in hand.

Stuart, who had also risen to his feet, was staring at him between sullen and mocking, without taking his eyes off the coldness of the gunslinger. He was trying to read in advance his reaction to what might happen, but after those seconds of explosion, Foot's gaze revealed nothing of what he pretended to know.

Foot ended up stating:

"I find it hard to believe that this could have happened like this.

Stuart dryly replied:

"You are deceiving a lady, who is also your friend, and I do not find you very gallant, Mr. Foot. I did it as they tell you and whenever I want I would repeat it again.

Foot, in a fit of rage, raised his hand quickly to his waist, at the same time he shouted:

"Well prove it.

But before his revolver was fully out of its holster, the black barrel of Stuart's gun was sinking into his chest, leaning sinisterly against it:

"I could prove it to you, as you see; but I don't want to, unless I continue to insist on that attitude.

The famous gunman widened his eyes and stood tense with his arm half bent. Not a single muscle in his face altered, and as Stuart continued in that threatening posture, he asked:

What do you expect?

"Any. My proof was theoretical only. I have nothing against you at the moment and ... I am not interested in your life, even though I know you would have shot me if you were faster than me.

Foot withdrew his hand from the gun, putting it back in its holster, and Stuart followed suit.

Agnes's made-up face had not contracted for a single moment during the agonizing moments of that dramatic scene. She was almost certain that one of them was going to fall, and yet she remained impassive. Despite himself, Stuart's calm, cold-bloodedness and skill in drawing his weapon had impressed him.

"Come on, Foot," he said, smiling as he rested his slender hand on the gunman's shoulder. " It would have caused me great annoyance to see either of you fall. You are too impetuous and I did not call you to do these scenes here or to force others to do them. My duty was to inform you faithfully of what happened and if you had common sense you would admit that it was Fred's fault, because you knew him well.

Foot took the bottle of whiskey with a calm pulse and filled his glass, draining it. Then he said:

"I think you're right, Agnes. I've been stupid getting on my nerves over something that didn't deserve it. The one who deserved that this man had shot me is me.

"Why should he?

"Well ... because if you weren't so fast and ahead of me, I would have fired. You have caused me damage that you cannot assess.

Stuart, smiling cynically, stated:

"I like you for your honesty, but I don't hold a grudge against you. He knew that would be his reaction and he was prepared to avoid it. As for the damage, maybe we can fix it.

"How?

"There is a saying that goes: 'A dead king, set king.' Why can't I replace Fred on your crew?

"You? Who are you to aspire to that?

"Hell of hell! I have already told you my name, you have seen the rest, and if something is missing I will add that my record of service in the world may not detract from next to yours. Of course, this does not mean anything, because what it is about is to show that it is used or not for what it is intended.

"You seem too ambitious to me," Foot objected.

"Don't believe it, in this case, my ambition is minimal. If I were to consider myself as ambitious as you judge me, I would aspire not to the position of Fred, but to supplant him in his activities, and without vanity I can affirm that I have never failed to achieve what I have proposed.

"Sometimes you fail in life.

"That can happen to anyone ... even you.

"So far I have not failed.

"Neither do I, but I think this discussion is idle. I have made a proposal and you have to decide. It is clear that if I killed his second it was because he wanted it and because he was a poor devil next to me. If this tells you something, take it into consideration, and if not, say it so that I can make up my own composition for myself.

Foot was thoughtful. Fred's death posed a problem for him, for he was a valuable man to him. Dead, he needed to replace him, but what would the others say? Some would consider themselves worthy to replace him. In spite of everything, he guessed in Stuart a very dangerous possible enemy, and if he tied him short and had him within reach of his hand, he could control him better than free.

At last it was decided.

"It is something to which at this moment I cannot answer. It is true that I am the boss and I impose my will on my men, but it would sow a schism if I imposed on a stranger without at least warning them and making them see that it can be a convenient thing for everyone. Still, I do not expect opposition to cease to exist.

"I am not interested in that opposition as far as I am concerned. If someone has to oppose something, let them tell me and oppose me. We'll work that out between the two of us.

"Too confident in yourself, stranger. That can lose you.

"If that happens, I will hold on. You decide and the rest matters little to me.

"Okay, come back here tomorrow night and I'll answer.

"Tomorrow he will have me here to find the answer.

Foot turned to Agnes, who hadn't been involved in the conversation, and looked at her intently. She smiled in amusement, and deep down she was. He had found in Stuart a man like no other he had hitherto known.

At last he said:

"Well, Agnes, this was a bit theatrical, it had never happened before; we will see how it ends. Then I'll send for Fred's body for my men to bury. After all, he served me loyally.

"Sounds good to me, Foot. For the rest, I will celebrate that you are fixed and that you are lucky.

He waved goodbye and left the rooms of "California Beauty", being dismissed by Stuart with an enigmatic smile. He was sure he had won a decisive trick for him. Foot would think about it, and as a lesser evil, he would end up accepting him in his band. Then ... the devil would have the last word.

CHAPTER VI

HOW THE BIG NIGHT ENDED

As soon as he reached his lair, Foot dispatched one of the men who made up his personal guard to find his gang members and meet him. They all had to walk around the premises of their demarcation and it would not be difficult to locate them.

And so, around two in the morning, sixteen hardened and dangerous men, for whom life or death was a mere accident among the many of their long career of undesirables, found themselves reunited with Foot, overcome with curiosity to know the object of that untimely call. Fred's death was no longer a mystery to them, because the rumor had spread throughout the underworld district and everyone imagined that the call would be to give them an official account of the event, and what was logical, also to name a substitute.

Being second in Foot's band "and in any other" was a firm step for at any moment of commotion to be able to occupy his position if the boss, who was not invulnerable because he was, fell in the fight as so many others had fallen and had to replace it.

Perhaps the one with the most hope of promotion, Fred gone, was Adair Jessup. He was considered one of the most audacious, fearsome and selfish of the gang, and therefore, as soon as he learned of the disappearance of his rival, he considered that the one who had the most right to replace him was him.

Thus, when Foot gave them an account of the event and how it had developed, Jessup asked:

"What have you thought to do with the guy who sent you to hell, boss?

"What are you talking about?

"Simply, if he intends to leave Fred's death without avenging.

Foot looked at him coldly and replied:

"I don't have to set out to avenge anyone's death when a guy like Fred stupidly seeks it out and falls for a fool. My men can fall into a fight "mine" and fall for any circumstance; So they have me by their side for that and whatever is necessary, but if someone, from man to man, boasts of bravo and then does not show it and falls, it does not serve me. Is this clear?

Well, maybe yes. But if Fred was drunk it wasn't difficult to show off fast with him.

"Whoever did it would have sent Fred to hell drunk and not drinking. I know the kind of man he is.

"Do you know him?

"I didn't know him, but it took me a very short time to get to know him. When I admitted you, Jessup, I did not know you, but I was not wrong in judging you. The same thing happens with that man.

"Then...

"So, I have decided something and for that I have brought you together. The guy is something special, worthy of a gang as tough as ours, and since he has come to San Francisco to make himself known and earn money, I have decided not to let him roam for his respects and have him by my side. I would not like a new Fritt to emerge to disturb the now quiet life that we lead, and before he goes over to the other side or raises his head on his own, I have stayed with him.

Jessup, not wanting to openly oppose his boss's decisions, exclaimed:

"Well, I think it's not a bad idea. If we have had a loss, someone has to cover it, and if the guy deserves it, that one is as good as another; Have you hired him yet?

"Yes.

"Was it okay?

"Yes, it has seemed good to him as long as I give him the position that Fred occupied, and it seemed to me that it works for him. Are there any who are not satisfied?

They all looked at each other in amazement. They did not accept that he decided to grant him that position of trust, when he had among his men many capable of supplying the dead.

"I'm not satisfied" Jessup dared to proclaim when he saw that none of his companions dared to raise their voices against it.

"For what reason?

"Because what he can do I can do, and not just me, but any of my teammates.

"Even confront him?

"You don't even wonder about that.

"Agree. As I am determined to admit him, I do not want to do it without giving others the same possibilities as him. If you are willing to dispute the position, it will be for you if you win it. As that man is worth a lot and I do not disdain him, or suppress him, or attract him to my side; but because it is worth it and it can be very useful to me, I am not willing to suppress it in any way.

Whoever is not satisfied will have to send him to hell face to face to show that he is superior to him, and if he manages to make him bite the dust, I will not oppose anything, but if he fails, he will end up convincing me that he was worth more than Fred and that whoever tries dispute his position. You are the first to try it, and if someone else thinks like you will follow you in the test if you fall, but if you win, you will be second in the squad. We agree?

There were new looks from the gunmen. Fred was a good revolver and dead that one, Jessup could be considered the best. If he did not serve to eliminate the intruder, none considered themselves as fast as Jessup.

Finally, one came forward to answer:

"Why more tests, boss? We are all sure that Jessup will know how to do it very well. If you try, that's enough.

"Compliant. Anyway, I'm not so stupid that I allowed you to try one by one and that you were falling in a stupid way. I consider all of you skilled with the colt in hand, and if that stranger takes the lead first, he'll be better than the rest for me. I do not want to impose it on you capriciously, but with reasons of ... lead. If Jessup falls, you will accept him as my right arm and I will not tolerate any more arguments or rebellions. I know that it will be a very valuable element if, for any reason, the fight is resumed and we have to fight like wild beasts again.

"When are we going to measure that tiger? Jessup asked mockingly.

"Tomorrow night I have arranged to see him and give him the answer. I will meet you in the same place and we will agree on the place and time of the meeting. This is all I had to tell you.

"Well, if you don't regret it ... After I talk to him, we'll see each other.

"I hope you both don't regret it" was Foot's reply.

The gang left their lair to disperse through the village. Forming small groups, each one chose the gambling den where to finish the rest of the night and exchange impressions about the strange event.

Jessup, with two of his closest friends from the gang, reached the street of San Francisco bitterly discussing the event. The gunman, excited, did not agree to wait so many hours because he felt angry at the delay that he did not think he deserved. He was one of the oldest men in the gang, who had been in serious danger helping Foot, and now he had a deep disdain for a leader whom he considered too fickle and impressionable.

Enraged, he stopped commenting:

"That's a bitch from Foot, don't you think?

"At least it is giving ourselves little importance. I know of some revolver freaks and I don't think that guy is superior to them. We are not crippled.

"No, of course we are not," Jessup yelled, "nor do we have lead in our hands, and I wonder why we have to wait until tomorrow to solve this matter. If, as Foot has said, he is at Agnes's place, by going there and killing him, the matter can be solved without wasting all that stupid time. The dilemma is with him or suppress him, because he is suppressed and in peace.

"Yes, but you have also heard him clearly say that whoever does it will have to do it face to face. Let's not complicate things further by sowing the weeds, because if he found out that we were suppressing him between the three of us, he will think that we have been afraid of him and he can do without us. The things are not to be self-employed and Fritt would laugh a lot at the schism and even take advantage of the disunity.

Jessup, beside himself, bellowed;

"I don't need you at all. To send him to hell if we find him there, I am enough.

"That's fine" replied his partner "; but look well how you do it. Agnes will inform the boss of how the encounter will unfold, and if he is not satisfied with how you behave, you will not have gained anything by doing it.

"Yes, yes, I understand you. I must go in, ask for him, tell him who I am, warn him that I am going to kill him and ask him to shoot five times before I draw the gun so that no one will say that I did not let him take the initiative, right?

"Don't overdo it, Jessup," one of his companions replied. Remember that Fred spoke less and pretended to do more and you saw. As long as no one accuses you of having shot without warning you have enough.

"Well, follow me. I am looking for him, and if I find him, you will witness how the fight will unfold. I'm not half drunk like Fred was when he did that nonsense.

The two undesirables shrugged and followed him. They could not deny that it was their pleasure for Jessup to prove himself faster and safer than Fred, and therefore more than the stranger, but if he failed, neither was willing to intervene in breach of orders.

* * *

Stuart, seemingly unhurried, had stayed in Agnes's rooms. When Foot had disappeared he sat down again, filled one of the glasses with whiskey, and settled back in the armchair.

Agnes, with a special smile, commented:

"You are not very gallant, Stuart, I drink too.

"Oh, excuse me. I thought the fright hadn't passed yet and that her pretty throat wouldn't admit anything through it.

"Who the hell told you that I was scared?

"It was not so? Excuse me then; It turns out that you have more nerve than I had expected. Or is it that you don't think I was about to kill that guy?

"Of course I have not believed it.

"For what reason?

"Well, because he judged you so vain, that you are not able to take advantage of the slightest advantage in your favor, so that no one misinterprets you, and this time you yourself have confessed that you had all the advantages in your favor.

Stuart laughed with amusement and stated:

"You win, Agnes. You are a woman of wonderful intuition. So it was, but that toad does not trust too much because I am a man of manias. If he repeated his luck, he would not let him draw it again. What do you suspect you can decide?

"Well ... that will stay with you.

Even if your men oppose it?

"Even so. He has taken the measure well and knows how much you can be worth to him. You will find a way to convince them if they protest.

"I'm not so sure. If there is strong opposition, you may leave it up to your men to decide the matter more simply.

"How? I do not understand you.

"Playing the ignorant if some or some try to suppress the competition. I know my people to know well the foot that can limp.

"Me too, and I know Foot is just as stupidly vain as you are. I would not authorize them out of pride in preventing someone from calling you a "coward" by suppressing you for not standing up to you or your men.

"They can do it without your consent.

"I don't dare say no, but in anticipation it is you who must guard yourself until you receive Foot's reply.

"How am I going to save myself if I don't know any of them? I'll stay here until the store closes.

She corrected the claim.

"Not here precisely. Not that I care about your presence, but I don't want anyone to misinterpret my hospitality to you. There are many who aspire to something from me, and if I have shown talent in something, it has been by treating everyone in such a way that no one believes he or she has more right than another nor more postponed than others. Foot himself is seriously in love with me for whatever reason and has not managed to get me to treat him better or worse than others in this area. I do very well this way and I avoid complications and responsibilities.

"I want to understand it. That is called flirtation.

Practical flirtation if you like.

"And I think you do well. Each is administered as you see fit. I have to confess that as I treat you, I like you more.

"Don't flatter me, I'm going to fade. The one who likes you is Betty.

"I have a heart capable of admitting a few smaller ones than mine.

"But mine is too big a gauge to fit in a cage like that full of weird beats. I would not admit annoying friction.

"Well, let's not talk any more about that matter, which does not seem to please him. How is Betty?

"I think if you let her rest for tonight she will win a lot. I think you do not have the ears to listen to your wooing with serenity.

"For my part, have a rest. There are very pretty girls downstairs with whom I can happily kill time ... Do you want to toast with me? Since you called me to order earlier, I will rectify my rudeness.

Stuart filled their glasses by offering him one. Then the glass collided.

"For the most suggestive and clever woman I have ever met in all the West," stated Stuart.

"For the only man in whom I would ever care if he were capable of such a thing," Agnes replied.

"Thanks. That makes me more proud than anything Foot has to offer.

"You are good at it. Because if you raise your wings too high he is a good hunter and could offer you an ounce of lead in them. Don't keep drinking just in case.

"Thank you for the advice, which I will try to follow... Ah, a plea! If you observe something strange, let me know as you can, even if it is by sending me a kiss with the tips of your fine fingers that look like ten fine butterflies with pink wings. I'm not sure all of them until Foot decides to officially introduce me to his men.

"Well, I'll be taking care.

They descended into the living room. This one, packed with the public, was in the middle of the maelstrom. The roulette wheel was in full swing and an exciting Pharaoh game had been established, with the clientele watching for the exciting plays. Perhaps for this reason, Stuart's new presence went almost unnoticed, and few noticed the couple as they descended the sumptuous staircase.

When they reached the salon, Stuart took a look around and noting that the girls were all engaged to various clients, he changed his mind and decided to try his hand at roulette. That night he considered himself a man of fortune and wanted to see how far it would go.

Standing behind the points that occupied the seats, he began to place the chips he had exchanged. Fortune, as he trusted, began to smile at him and half an hour later he was making a few hundred dollars.

Agnes, besieged by some good customers, sat down with them at the table she always kept reserved for her use. It was a magnificent observatory to keep track of the revolving door and control everyone who entered or left the gambling den.

Until around one o'clock, his eyes took on a special sparkle when he discovered three stragglers who had just entered. It was Jessup and his two companions, and from the way they looked around the room, especially the first of them, he guessed that their presence there was not accidental, but that they came with a preconceived purpose.

Requesting permission from his companions, he got up and scurrying between the tables managed to get to the side of the adventurer, very entertained in following the capricious turns of the ivory ball. She nudged him on the elbow and murmured:

"Stuart, stop playing and keep an eye on those three guys standing near the door. They belong to Foot's gang and I can't tell myself if their visit is accidental or premeditated.

"Thanks. My heart was telling me that something like this could happen. Don't worry, they won't surprise me.

"Be careful, above all, with the tallest one in the middle of the group. His name is Jessup and he is one of the most dangerous and unscrupulous men in the whole gang.

She walked around the table casually as if interested in keeping an eye on the incidents of the game, and when she left it she started walking towards the door as if she had not noticed the presence of the three undesirables.

At that moment, Jessup's two companions separated from him, taking their seats at a table that had just been vacated, while Jessup, standing, wandered his gray and evil eyes around the room, as if trying to discover on his own who he was and where was the one he was looking for.

Agnes, smiling and serene, after giving the notice to the stranger, advanced towards Jessup and, staring at him, asked:

"Hi Jessup, what are you doing there freaking out? Can't you find a seat where you can be comfortable?

"Does that interest you very much, Agnes?

"No, but I think that if you were in your bed you would be much better than here. The cold that blows tonight is very dangerous for certain temperaments like yours.

"My bones are very tough against those kinds of temperatures, Agnes, you should know. Not even lead handled with a treacherous hand is capable of finishing me off as it did with Fred.

"Depending on where you blow from and how you blow, Jessup. You forget that men as stubborn as you, better than you, with a gun in hand and with more cartel of thugs lie softly in our cemetery, including Fred.

"Fred was stupid and drunk. I'm smarter and haven't had a drink.

"I wasn't drunk Jessup, I can assure you because I checked. You better go home or visit other places more cheerful than this. I didn't think Foot was capable of concocting things that would discredit him in the eyes of the people.

The gunman bristled, replying:

"To hell Foot! It has nothing to do with this, which is my personal business. Someone has killed Fred, who was my friend, and I want to know where he is and if he can do the same to me.

"Is it enough for you that I assure you that I would do the same? You already know that I know men well and I know what almost all of them are capable of giving of themselves. Having seen how "your friend" fell, I can assure you. I did not know that you had so much love for him now that he can no longer overshadow you

Jessup, irritated by the piercing ironies of Agnes, whom he hated for her haughtiness and aggressiveness, growled:

"What are you talking about, repainted parrot? Get out of the way of men and stay out of their stuff. You're misleading Foot, and if I take Fred's position, I think the thing about you being the only one who doesn't trade like the others is going to end.

Agnes, furious, replied:

"If I was a man, I would have slapped you or put an ounce of lead in your mouth to end your bragging. If Foot had the bad taste and tact to name you his second, he would forbid him and you from coming in here, and he would not pay a single penny. To defend myself and to defend my business I have enough and I am enough. Or do you think I'm unguarded waiting for a guy like you to come threaten me?

"Do not throw challenges, because I do not admit them, damn your old bones" roared Jessup in exasperation. I've come to kill that guy to replace Fred later, and when I've sent him to hell we'll see if Foot continues to be silly and doesn't force you to contribute. You will have a lot of trouble with all of us if you don't.

"I'm afraid he doesn't have any, if you have to be the one to ask them. How do you want to kill him, from behind, when he is asleep, or do you want him to be tied so that he does not scare you when you draw?

"Me with those? I am too much of a man to get rid of him face to face and without advantage.

"And those two who accompany you, what will they do?

"They have nothing to do with this matter. They will be mere spectators no matter what, as I have invited them to witness the duel.

"I don't know you, Jessup. Are you really willing to act like a man?

"Let that guy come out of the hole where he's hiding and show his face. Then I'll show you.

At that moment, Stuart, who had advanced to stand with his back against one of the central columns and his cigarette dangling from his lip, said with a frosty accent:

"Go away, Agnes, nothing goes with you. I've heard enough bravado and nonsense to make me bored. I'm waiting for you, Jessup.

He said it loudly and with a hurtful accent. The customers, hearing him, turned their heads tense and dozens of pairs of eyes fixed on the couple.

Stuart, leaning lightly on the spine, had his left arm leaning against it, his cigarette stubbed out on his thin, mocking lips, his right arm flaccid along his body. His eyes possessed a strange light of mockery and amusement, and his malicious little lights produced in Jessup an uncontrollable discomfort and rage, because in his long experience as a gunman he had contemplated and scrutinized many eyes when it came to defending himself and he knew those that were malicious and mocking. they made their owners more fearsome.

That moment of hesitation seemed like a late sign of regret, something like a voice warning him that he had over-judged someone he did not know in advance and that it was best to back off.

But it was too late to do so. Nothing more humiliating for him than a retraction in front of so many people, when his mouth had been a dump of threats and foolish presumptions.

He had to hold the type and there was no other solution. He knew his enemy was waiting for the slightest move of his to imitate him and he was pondering whether he could actually be faster than him pulling the colt. It was brief seconds that he hesitated, although to him it seemed like a century because of the multitude of reflections that had been taking place in such a short time. He had to resolve this dramatic situation once and for all, and finally he made up his mind.

His arm bent to his waist quickly and his fingers hooked on the butt of the weapon. She knew that once imprisoned she would come out smoothly and there would no longer be anyone who could avoid her deadly effects.

He did it with dizzying speed, although it seemed to him that it had taken him endless minutes to do it, but when he felt the free movement of her hand he breathed in savage glee and flexed his arm again to fire.

Everything was as fast as his own thought, which seemed to follow the performance of his arm period by period, and yet it achieved nothing. As the gun straightened to fire, he felt his arm shake as if a hole had exploded in it, and the hand seemed to have unexpectedly penetrated a red-hot brazier. He heard an explosion, but with distant vibrations, and then another. This time to feel in his stomach as if a fiery arrow had penetrated until it pierced his spine.

And it fell like a mass after several seconds of miraculously standing upright, while swaying grotesquely before falling.

This time there were no shouts from the customers, no murmurs or comments. Only an anguished and solemn silence, something that seized the throats and sent chills through the marrow, for all had seen how the strange stranger had dangerously recreated himself in allowing his enemy to reach his hand to his side before he began any movement.

And yet it had been faster. His first projectile, undoubtedly as a precaution, was directed at his opponent's hand, destroying it and making it useless for aggression, since the revolver was projected into the air, and the second directed it at his stomach. Deadly shot and he sure had no escape.

But Stuart didn't holster. He stood with the tense colt waiting for the reaction of the two companions of the dead man, but they, with their hands resting on the tabletop and somewhat pale with emotion, did not dare to make a move.

Agnes turned to them to ask:

"What do you guys plan to do now?

One of them replied:

"Go report to the boss what happened. We came only because Jessup made us do so. Foot has not intervened in this, because he told him to wait until tomorrow, that he would arrange the duel loyally. Jessup wanted to replace Fred and did not admit him as second.

"Well then, go ahead and give him an account of what happened. It is better for everyone.

And the two gunmen left the premises watched by "the Californian Beauty" and by Stuart, who did not lose sight of them until he saw them leave.

CHAPTER VII

A DANGEROUS WOMAN

Agnes was not willing to allow her house to become the anteroom or storage room of the cemetery, so she ordered her men to take Jessup's body and remove it from the premises. He had already retained Fred's body out of consideration for his friend Foot, but the case could not be repeated. It was enough that this and some other times the men had been shot through the middle of the room, staining the parquet and causing the consequent damage.

When the establishment was cleaned again, Stuart, realizing the shows he had given in the joint, commented:

"I'm afraid I shouldn't be coming around here much, Agnes. I am causing him some disturbances and the devil knows well that was not my intention, nor that I have caused them for pleasure.

"Don't worry," she said, laughing sarcastically, "Scenes like this have developed many in this house, as in others of its kind. It is a tribute from which we are not exempt, although I must admit that I had not seen anyone writhing on the ground like a lizard in a long time, nor had he smelled of gunpowder either.

Stuart, who feared further retaliation from Foot's gang, said:

"I think the best thing I can do is leave. I will prevent these events from repeating themselves.

She took him by the shoulders and said:

"Don't be in a hurry, Stuart. Sit down and have a drink.

She took him to her table, where she made him sit down, while ordering them to give him a drink. Then he excused himself for a moment and went up to the floor.

It was already very late and the noise in the living room would gradually subside. Agnes went to the bedroom, where she had left Betty. She was still lying on the bed of "California Beauty" and seemed less nervous.

"How are you feeling, girl? Agnes asked.

"Good, pretty good. I think I'm in a position to get up and go back to ...

"Needless. It's too late, Betty.

"Has something happened down there? The girl asked fearfully.

"Why you ask?

"Well ... because I thought I heard shots and ...

"Do not worry. It was a slight fight of the many that are provoked. I think if you are fit, you can go home. It is already very late and it is not worth it that you return to the room for half an hour.

"If you don't think it is convenient ...

"Yes, it is better for your nerves.

The girl got up. She was still pale and limp with emotion. While fixing her messy hair, she asked a question:

"Do you think that ... something will happen to that man for having intervened in ...?

"Don't worry about him, Betty, and forget about him. I have already settled this matter with Foot and nothing will happen, but ... I think it is in your best interest and for everyone not to be too impressed by this man. You know that I do not like girls for my business who allow themselves to be dominated without restraint by a man. Apart from the fact that they are distracted and do not fulfill their mission with joy and without sentimental coercion, there is the disadvantage of the pressure that they exert on you, inhibiting you and damaging my business.

»I hope you realize what I advise you, because I appreciate you and I would feel that I had to do without you as I did without others that you already know.

Betty, stammering, replied:

"Yes, yes, ma'am. I realize it and I will try to please her.

"That is very vague. To try is not to be sure of doing it. You must not be impressed and continue as you were. You know that I, as a woman, know how to treat you well and that in no other place would you be pampered as I do. Apart from the fact that there is no owner here who tries to impose himself on you. Take care of your job if you don't want to foolishly roll from one to another.

Betty finished rearranging the order of her headdress a bit and started to leave. When he was going to go out to the gallery to go down to the gambling den, Agnes intervened, blocking his path and warned:

"No, not there. Get out this other way, because there is no need for them to see you. They better continue to believe that you are resting from the emotion.

Betty didn't seem very happy with the order. He would have liked to see Stuart again, even if it was in passing, and thank him for his courageous intervention, but after Agnes's warnings he did not dare to rebel.

Humbly he went out through the door that communicated through a corridor with the reserved staircase isolated from the gambling den. Agnes, too solicitous, accompanied her to the door, advising her:

"Bundle up well because the night has gotten too cold. If you're not feeling well tomorrow, let me know, and you can take a couple of days off. I will pay you the salary as if you had acted and with the others I will be able to fix myself well.

"Thank you very much, you are very kind, but I am not feeling bad. The scare is over and I will be able to perform tomorrow.

"Whatever you want. Goodbye, Betty.

Agnes took the promise equivocally and stood at the door watching her go, until she vanished into the shadows of the road. When she was sure that he would never return, she went up to her rooms again, contemplated herself in the mirror, flirtatiously arranging her curly hair, carefully rearranged her makeup, although it had not decomposed, and went back down the gallery stairs to the den .

Because of this feline maneuver, Stuart had not heard of Betty's departure and was hoping to see the girl when she left. This was the reason why he accepted Agnes's invitation and stayed despite the lateness of the hour.

"The Californian Beauty" sat down next to him and invited him to drink again. He supported him by raising his glass to toast him and with skill he was entertaining him, while the customers were marching by little by little, until only the laggards were left, to whom it was necessary to warn that it was going to close.

It was early morning when Stuart, tired, got up, saying:

"I must go, Agnes. I am exhausted.

She, smiling suggestively, commented:

"Yes, you look a little tired, Stuart, and you should rest. Wait some minutes.

He looked at her in alarm. This sudden confidence in him seemed highly suspicious and he was on his guard.

Agnes called the manager and gave him the order to close. Then, turning to Stuart, he pleaded:

"Do you want to accompany me upstairs for a moment?

Stuart hesitated. It felt like stepping forward with overconfidence and finding himself entangled in a subtle mesh that held him back.

He was about to refuse, but then, believing that he was inviting him upstairs to say goodbye to Betty, he accepted. He felt a special attraction for the girl and would like to know if she had calmed down. Perhaps Agnes meant to beg him to accompany her, and this would be nice to him.

When they reached the cabinet, Agnes indicated an armchair, saying:

"Sit down and have a drink. That will tone you up.

Again that tuteo made him feel bad in the ear. He was beginning to get alarmed and decided not to accept the seat. He just filled the glass, saying:

"I'm fine on my feet. Tell me what you want, Agnes.

She, trying to hide her anger, asked:

"How violent are you next to me?" I don't think I'm a person who eats children raw.

"I passed from childhood a long time ago, Agnes. It is not women's teeth that I am afraid of.

"What are you afraid of them then?

"To his lips.

"Very gallant. I thought it was the least scary thing.

"Me. As many times as I let myself be seduced by them, so many times that I was on the verge of failure. If in normal times I was suspicious, this is not my best time to forget the lessons learned.

"Does that mean in a devious way that you find me unattractive to you?

He understood that there was a hidden threat background to the question and many thoughts with a view to the future crossed his imagination. He had been able to see what that woman weighed in San Francisco, especially among the underworld people, and more specifically in Foot's spirit, and he did not want to put himself in front of her as an enemy and a spiteful woman. She might still be of use to him, until she was a power freed from all fear, and he quickly responded by advancing on her.

"Listen, Agnes; I am not lying to you if I tell you that I find in you the greatest attractions that I have found in few women. From the first moment I have believed that you were an exception to the rule in that sense and you have attracted me like few others, but I would like you to understand me. I know myself. If pretty eyes cross my path and I allow myself to be dazzled by them, I am a lost man, at least until I wake up from sleep. I do nothing to the right and I even forget that there may be two steps from me the mouths of some colts waiting for me to drive the lead from my back.

"I have had the opportunity to study you and have come to believe that you could drive me crazy, which I have never disliked when it comes to women, but this time instinct tells me to wait. I do not disdain you, on the contrary, I think we would make an excellent couple of demons in this hell full of flames, but I would like us to form it when we are above its boilers and there is no fear that we will burn ourselves in them.

"I have come with a determined purpose that I do not give up for nothing. Give me the precise time to conquer San Francisco by my own means, and when I am the owner of it ... open your arms and close them so as not to let go of me, but let those revolvers that can now threaten my life be her safeguard. Then I will not mind closing my eyes and not looking back knowing that nothing threatens me.

She listened to him tense and stared at him. She had thought him a strange man, but he was finding it more than he thought, and in that silent but intense examination, he seemed to be drilling him to the bottom of his soul, to know if he was lying to him or really speaking with rude sincerity.

Finally he answered:

"Listen, Stuart; I am a woman who has flown over all human passions, because I have never found the exceptional man who would make the hidden string of sentimentality vibrate in me. There are many here who believe they are exceptional because they are wild and blind beasts who know how to handle a revolver and believe that this is the supreme exception.

No, it's not that, and I've never been moved. The man that I have longed for and could not find must have other strange qualities, which in a few hours I have found in you, and you have been the one who has arrived when I was tired of waiting. I would like you to realize that and speak to me sincerely and not deceive me.

I can do a lot for you and against you, but I am a loyal friend or enemy. I want you to be the same and know on what plane we can unite or fight. You are on time and you are the one who must decide.

He, unaffected by the threat, replied:

"I have told you what I had to say, Agnes. For now, I wish I had no complications other than those that the environment could create for me. Let me solve them without having my mind occupied with things that would distract me. When it's all over, we'll talk about this.

"It's okay, Stuart. In that case, go away. This door is open for you any time you want to come. I hope I never have to tell you otherwise.

"Don't worry, sweetie, you won't tell me," he said.

He came over and gave her a kiss. Then, with a gentle greeting, he stepped back saying:

"Rest, Agnes, and see you tomorrow.

He left through the reserved part of the joint. Agnes followed him with a bright gaze until she saw him disappear, then she sank back into the chair, her face tense.

She filled the same glass in which Stuart had drunk with whiskey and, draining it in small sips, she indulged in a hissing monologue, in which, free of witnesses, she put all the nerve and the will that she was possessed with.

"I like him," he said, "I like him because he doesn't look like anyone I have dealt with so far. I like it and I will not allow anyone to take it from me. I do not know if he wants to deceive me or is sincere when speaking. Be that as it may, I am a woman who does not give up when she yearns for something, and if she tried to play games with me ... as Agnes is my name, she would remember me forever. I am a woman, but with courage and cruelty, nobody wins me. I would make life miserable for him and ... I am even capable of killing him despite his mastery of weapons. "

And throwing the glass with a slap, he went to his bedroom to indulge in a rest that that night was to be more than rest, a terrible restlessness.

* * *

When Stuart woke up the next day, he was extremely thirsty and had a dry, harsh palate. He had drunk more than usual and the emotions he had suffered last night had taken their toll on him.

He promised not to abuse the drink in the future. Things were not enough to see his faculties diminished at a time when his future was being gambled on a very indecisive card.

The water in the brass jug was ice cold. The night had been harsh and the liquid accused him. He filled the basin and beat himself hard. The coolness of the water restored some of his energy.

And with them came to his thoughts, above all else, the figure of Agnes.

What a strange woman! He "mumbled." It would be nice if he really had a crush on me! It is a contingency that I had not thought about and in which now I have to think carefully. "

He had lived so long in such a short time that he knew the value of those fleeting adventures, but he also knew of certain temperaments, too dangerous to be frivolously dismissed when it came to touching the consequences.

And he was not willing to chain his life to "California Beauty" because he considered her too strong a dish for his delicate stomach. She was too wise and willful a woman, who could complicate his frivolous existence, and what he needed right now was freedom of action, the freedom to maneuver at will and carry out his ambitious plans.

To these considerations it was necessary to add others. He was sure of joining Foot's gang and couldn't ignore that Foot had a crush on Agnes. If for whatever reason she found out that he had crossed her path, even without intending it, things were going to get too complicated and it could be a disservice to both of them.

And finally, without realizing it, he remembered Betty. This was indeed a woman who attracted him of her own free will and not by imposition of the whims of others. She did not disdain that on the moral ground perhaps she was neither better nor worse than Agnes, but it was quite another matter. A woman who would allow herself to be dominated, but who would not try to dominate him as "California Beauty."

He had to clarify positions. If the matter did not go to greater, he would have nothing to oppose, but if she had made more extensive calculations, the case was going to be wrong to harmonize their relationships. He knew what she could weigh as a spiteful woman and was more afraid of a woman in such conditions than a man with a colt in his hand.

Finally he dressed and went down to breakfast in the dining room. After doing so, he took to the street strolling to the caress of the morning sun, and without realizing it, instinctively, he entered the main street.

Agnes's joint was closed. He was glad and tried to pass by. By then at night he would have time to reflect and make a decision about Agnes.

But he had barely advanced a few steps, when he discovered her tapping on the false sidewalks. She wore a gaudy rose-colored gown with large ruffles and frilly sleeves snugly at the wrists, and the high lace collar fitted her still shapely throat.

She covered her hair with a hat with a very high brim at the front and falling at the sides, which was adjusted to her throat by a silk ribbon, while her hands, which were balancing the silk bag, appeared covered up to the elbow by the mitten gloves of lace.

Even though she was no longer a girl, she was still attractive and eye-catching. She was a wise woman, who knew how to enhance her mature charms with mischief and distinction.

When she discovered Stuart, she smiled gracefully and he responded to the smile in the same way, advancing towards her and discovering himself comically.

"May the Queen of San Francisco allow me to kiss your hand?"

"I like kisses tastier, Stuart.

"We would cause a scandal in this modest city if I dared to kiss you on the mouth in the middle of the street. Shall we leave it for privacy?

"We'll save it for your time, Stuart.

"Oh, that gives me chills with excitement. Such a placid and submissive little woman to a man; But tell me, is it that you come to break hearts through the streets of the wild city? Because you are not going to tell me that you are such a good devotee that you come from mass.

"I will go to church the day I do it with your arm.

"That day they will have to widen the door of the cathedral so that we can pass. I will be thinking of recommending that they widen the door. Where do you come from, cutie?

"To work for your cause, dear. I needed to clear up last night and know what Foot was thinking. I wasn't quite sure that he had no involvement in the Jessup affair and I wanted to clarify it. Fortunately, everything is ready. Jessup was ahead of the events and it was all his doing nothing more.

"Glad to hear... for both of us.

"You will also be glad to hear that Foot has decided to give you Fred's position and is expecting you in an hour to make your presentation to his men. I was thinking of going to your hotel to let you know.

"Have you gone to ask him to do so? He asked with a harsh voice.

"I swear I do not. It was something decided by him since last night to give you that position. I just went to make sure there had been no cheating.

"That's something else and I appreciate your good offices, but I don't like women becoming my babysitters.

"You seem too proud, Stuart, and you forget that a woman, especially like me, has strength.

"I have mine and for these matters it is enough for me, Agnes. If you want us to be good friends, stay out of my business. You would lower me in the eyes of those people and you would complicate your life at the same time, which I do not want, because I want to avoid harm to you.

"Why was he going to complicate her? Now you have achieved a good position and
...

"That is not enough for me, I already told you. I aspire to be as much as anyone else, and the fact that I take advantage of that step to climb it does not mean that I stop in the middle of the ladder. I will climb to the top, pushing whoever is on top, and I will hold or fall, but I will not be halfway.

"What do you mean, you vain?

"That I don't give Foot more value than what she has to be the absolute owner of something. I aspire to supplant him a day more or less near and that is why I want you to remain on the sidelines. You would be involved in the fight and you would feel it. You seem to forget that he feels a lot for you and that if he suspects that you feel for me and I reciprocate ... do you realize the many things that could happen and none pleasant for everyone?

"That does not worry me. When I have wanted something I have fought for it without weighing the consequences.

"It is very heroic, that, but it has its drawbacks ... I think that for now it is better to forget about last night and postpone many things and wait for events without complicating them.

"Forget it? No. Postpone it? Well, but not for Foot ... for you if that's what interests you.

"I am interested because I want to choose the moment to show him that I care very little about his power, his fame and his courage.

"Don't be vain. You're getting things that ...

"That I have not sought, this is the truth," he refuted, "and that is why I do not want to accept more responsibilities than those that I seek for myself and not for others.

Agnes hardened the features of her pretty face.

For a long time, dozens of hard and soft, bold and timid, rich and poor, had besieged him unmoved by pleas, gifts, and threats, scorning them dryly and fearlessly.

And at that moment, when he had allowed himself to be influenced by the attraction of that adventurous type whom he hardly knew, but who had possessed the irresistible attraction of mastering his pride and stubbornness, he was haughty, dry and hard, despising or abusing that incipient passion that was beginning to burn his chest and for which many men would have laid their lives and fortune at his feet.

Furious, she advanced towards him, replying:

"If you're not interested, why that comedy last night? Why did you make me believe that ...?

He, realizing that it infuriated her and that it was not convenient for him to do so, softened and replied:

"Do not climb the tree interpreting my words in a way that is not true. It will be difficult for you to understand me, but it depends on your understanding that you get to do it. I want to tell you that I am not selling my independence of movement for anything or anyone. Outside of my personal performance, in the hours that I have nothing to dedicate time to myself, I will admit what you want, but nothing more than then.

»I want to know that I do not carry a burden on my back that could harm me, since the worry of having to defend myself from the front is enough. At the moment I am interested in Foot's friendship and joining his gang; I need to know the environment well to know where to move. Later, when I don't need him, it will be time to argue with him and see who of the two has more strength, but if you complicate it, I will lose all the possibilities, and to lose them it will be enough for him to feel angry for you and take me. between eyes. Do you want to understand it at once?

Agnes seemed reassured by this ambiguous explanation and replied:

"You mean that what interests you is that our friendship remains a secret … for now.

"Justly. And that in the eyes of the people you treat me as you would treat anyone else. Thus, I will be able to move freely, avoiding anticipating events.

"Well, if that is what you wanted to say, I will know how to wait for your good, but if at any time you need my help, do not hesitate to ask me.

»I want you to succeed in your projects and become what you aspire to in San Francisco. You have interested me precisely because you are an ambitious and fighting man for whom there are no borders, and you would disappoint me if you stopped halfway.

"Then no more talk. I will continue at my inn, I will see you in the joint at night as one more customer so as not to give rise to gossip that Foot could pick up to the detriment of both, and when the time comes, we will think about the future.

"Okay, Stuart. Now, go see Foot, who is waiting for you at home, Third Street, on the left, the last house.

Stuart breathed in relief when he found himself far from the joint.

Instinct told him that this was a dangerous trap for him and that if he couldn't find a way to get rid of its golden bars, one day he would be hunted in it like the most vulgar of birds.

CHAPTER VIII

A FULFILLED VISIT

Stuart and Foot's arrangement presented no major complications. After the extraordinary exploits of the first, no member of the gang was inclined to reject the adventurer's admission with the degree that the leader conferred on him, and Foot was satisfied to have at his side a man as hard and fast as that, that would be a solid guarantee for your personal safety and your future plans.

He personally took him that night to tour the demarcation assigned to him. He met gambling den owners, suspicious types with whom to be careful, he was given the names of the roughest elements that were loose in San Francisco, stubborn to work, albeit on a small scale, in the same environment as him. and Fritt had consolidated their fiefdoms, and soon he had the complete organization in his hands and he knew of the enormous stream of gold that daily went to the two hands of his new boss.

He had allocated ten percent of the total income to him. Considering that the crew was sixteen, and Foot was the boss, getting his fair half, his assignment was not negligible, but Stuart found it petty. Nevertheless, he accepted it. For the moment, he had his share left over, and the day he decided to aspire to more he would keep Foot's.

Days later he showed curiosity to meet the members of the opposing gang. As a tacit agreement, one and the other hardly frequented the opposing party's establishments to avoid possible complications, which would have turned the matter sour again, and Stuart justified the wish by saying that precisely in order to avoid any friction with the opposites he needed to know them personally and not from hearsay.

"Do you have a lot of interest in it? Foot had asked him.

"Yes, for two reasons: one, because neither of us are able to predict what might happen one day, and I don't like fighting ghost enemies; and another, because I am thinking that ... it would be more productive and comfortable to control all the stores and not have to share the income with anyone.

"Don't dream about it, Stuart" replied Foot "; I cherished that ambition for a long time and it cost me several months of fights, losing men and making them lose Fritt with no result other than exposing ourselves to spoiling the business for both of us. It is true that this way you earn less, but you win with rest and without danger.

"Perhaps the matter was not well focused," assured Stuart confidently. " There are blows that no one expects because of how audacious, and if a decisive one could be given well studied, we would lose nothing with it.

"Of course not, but it is very difficult. We are both well prepared not to be caught off guard.

"Okay, but by studying it better nothing is lost. Later it can be rejected or accepted, since they say that what two eyes cannot see can be seen by four. You have verified that I am not a man who is scared by many things.

"Okay, if not, you wouldn't be of my service; but for now we are going to leave things as they are.

"If it is your wish I say nothing, but that does not prevent me from introducing myself to Fritt.

"I'm going to do it, because I also think it is convenient for him to know that I have changed my trusted man and to know you well to avoid mistakes. We'll meet you at La Bola de Oro tonight at twelve. Come find me ... and if not, you'd better wait for me at Agnes's den. I want to greet her at the same time.

"Agree. At that time I will be there.

Stuart didn't like the rendezvous location. He had not appeared there for several days and he was not in the mood to hear reproaches and give false explanations about his absence. He had not gone because he did not want to, although later he tried to justify himself by claiming excessive work next to his new boss.

But that night, around eleven o'clock, he showed up at the joint. Agnes, who was enraged by the abandonment in which he had her, hastened to take him to her reserved table and harshly censured him:

"Is this the treatment I deserve, Stuart? You haven't been back here since the morning you went to see Foot.

"I couldn't, sweetie; ask your beloved torment and he will tell you.

"Foot is not my beloved torment and you know it. Do the favor of not spending ironies that I cannot bear.

"Forgives. It alluded to the interest that he has for you. I assure you that he has not left me a free moment, because we have been visiting all the gambling dens in his jurisdiction, so that he can meet the people and take charge of how he runs the business. Do not forget that now I am his trusted man and that all that I have to take him to heart. I hope you understand that now I am not dependent on myself alone.

"But a moment to come you will have had.

"I assure you, he did not leave me. Tonight I have been able to do it because he has summoned me here at twelve. He's taking me to meet Fritt.

"What interest do you have in meeting that guy?

"A lot, understand it. Isn't it fair and normal that I know my enemies more than my friends? One day unforeseen things might happen and I would risk running into him without knowing him. The thing would not be very happy for me and that is why I have asked him to introduce it to me.

"When are you going to finish and spend some time with me? You can come after you leave him.

"I would promise you if I knew we were going to find him soon and he won't entertain us much. But, anyway, I give you my word that as soon as I loosen my work a little and everything is normalized, I will come. We have little left.

Moments later the senator, Agnes's regular customer, appeared. This, although with regret, was forced to leave Stuart to attend to him.

The adventurer took advantage of that moment of respite to go over to greet Betty. He hadn't seen her since the night of his dramatic fight with Jessup and he missed her so much.

He approached the girl casually, saying:

"How are you, Betty? I guess your nerves will have completely calmed down by now.

She glanced at Agnes, which was not lost on Stuart, and replied:

"I'm fine thank you very much. I was sorry I could not thank you for your intervention then, but I take this moment to thank you.

"Bah! That didn't matter. A man should always come to the defense of a woman when he sees her run over, and much more if she is as pretty and attractive as you. Although I suppose they will not give me much free time, tonight I would like to dance with you.

"I'm sorry, but I'm engaged," the young woman apologized a little hesitantly. Agnes does not allow us to neglect her business and you must understand that. Another day may be.

He noticed that the girl was a bit nervous and thought he guessed that it was Agnes's presence. Frowning, he wondered if the girl knew anything about his flirtation with Agnes or if Agnes had given him some warning to curb his feelings.

She had to put him to the test, but not tonight. Twelve o'clock was close to ringing and Foot would soon make his appearance.

"Yes, another night will be" he said smiling "; but ... it will be that other night.

And he returned back to Agnes's table, not very satisfied with the interview with the young woman.

Californian Beauty, burning with the desire to be with Stuart for as long as possible, deftly managed to get rid of the clingy persona of the senator, leaving him very entertained at the roulette table. And sitting down next to Stuart, she stared at him, asking:

"What were you talking about with Betty?

He, realizing that the question contained an embers of poorly concealed jealousy, decided to make her rage a little and answered with irony:

"I was asking you if you knew what the weather would be like tomorrow. I'm afraid it might rain and since I'm a bit rheumatic ...

Agnes angrily bellowed in a low voice:

"Stuart, I don't take bad jokes. I hope you realize that secretly or not, there is a pact between the two and that I am not a woman who admits that another can cross my path.

He did not want to rush her patience and replied:

"Listen, Agnes, you can get old, but not jealous for no reason. The first would be better for you than the second. I asked her how she has been since the night of the fight and she took the opportunity to thank me for what I did. That was it.

"Everything, and it is quite a lot. Leave Betty behind, because she is a very attractive girl who knows how to captivate customers and is very useful for my business. I don't want you to spoil it or distract me.

"Understood, but I am also a customer, do you forget? And I need to be distracted like the others.

"If I am not attractive to distract you, alternate with the other girls. I think they are all pretty and nice.

"I will think about it, but it seems to me that you are imposing many conditions on me and that is not what we are talking about. If you trust yourself so much, why are you jealous of others?

"Because you have a very hard face. I promised not to get into your private business, but this is intimate and I have the right to do so.

"Let's not argue anymore, Agnes. It's ridiculous that we do it. There is Foot.

He got up to meet her, saying to Agnes:

"Sorry to leave you.

"Will you come back tonight?

"I already answered you. It is up to him and not me.

And he waved to join Foot and leave the joint with him.

They found Fritt at La Bola de Oro. Since he and Foot had signed the engagement, there had been no clash and both had not been modest in showing themselves in public in venues where the absolute owners were known. Nights were always the nightmare of the lawless, but that pact had softened the fear of plunging into darkness. What none had done yet was to go beyond their natural borders and visit the opposite field.

For this reason, Fritt was surprised when he saw Foot enter with a stranger.

Fritt rushed up from the table, indicating a seat before her.

"Go ahead, Foot," he said, "sit here. I am flattered to see you in these latitudes and I am ashamed that you were the first to take this step of true friendship.

They sat down next to him. At the table were three other individuals whose appearance denounced them as members of Fritt's gang and possibly the men he most trusted.

Fritt ordered the best whiskey and filled their glasses. Stuart had sat next to his boss, although the invitation was not received directly. They all drank slowly, as if studying the situation before speaking, and Foot, putting the glass on the tabletop, said:

"I did not want to come before, because the visit was not misinterpreted, but something has happened that has forced me to do so. Fred, my second, has died, and I thought it fair that, since we all know each other, you and your men know who is going to be my second. It is this one who accompanies me and his name is Stuart Sterling.

Fritt fixed his cold gray eyes on him and, extending his hand, white and slimy, said:

"So nice to meet you, Sterling. I've already heard something about you.

"That honors me," Stuart replied. It is always pleasant to know that the great figures are fixed in the small ones.

"Yes. They told me something about Fred's death and also about Jessup's. Two beautiful tasks if they were noble.

Stuart felt like a whiplash in his blood when he heard the comment and replied:

"You were saying that you had been informed about me. I see that it has not been like that ... or they have done it wrong.

"I did not see it and I can not comment on anything. What I know is from references, but I knew Fred and Jessup.

"He only needed to know me, and he already knows me.

"Justly. And I want to believe that when Foot has entrusted you with that position, it will be because he has good references from you and trusts your loyalty.

"The references that you have of me have simply been given to you by the facts. Was more needed?

"Not for him, since he admitted you to his side and is apparently glad he did.

"Of course I am," Foot was quick to affirm, who did not like the tone that the interview had acquired from the first moment.

"I'm not getting into it, Foot," said Fritt. Each one has its procedures to attend to its business.

Stuart, who did not like the reluctance of his opponent, commented:

"It seems to imply that you would have acted differently. That is not very flattering to me.

"That's how it is. I am very clear, but I do not try to get involved in anyone's things, and for my part I affirm that I am very distrustful by nature. My men have their history, but I know them thoroughly and I know how far they can go and how far I can control them. I have rejected very good men who, no matter how tough, did not serve me.

"I don't understand you," Stuart replied.

"I will explain it to you, and it is not that I conceptualize you in this case. There were men who, considering them too ambitious, I refused them. Those who know how to use a revolver well and are not afraid to use it are enough for me, but nothing more. I want arms that execute and not brains that think, because I think that if I think, that's enough.

Stuart grinned in amusement. Fritt was far more dangerous and subtle than Foot. He knew what he was up to and knew certain psychologies, which could be dangerous, but he replied softly:

"I would like to know what your men would do in certain circumstances, if their orders failed and measures had to be taken for the time being and regardless of them.

"Shoot or leave. I do not demand more of you.

"Good; I do not dispute it. I thought the second of a gang was the continuation of his boss. If not, I think the charge is unnecessary.

"I have it for luxury. I highlight one for being the most effective at the time of the fight and for conveying my orders concretely.

Stuart, who was beginning to lose patience at Fritt's insinuations, cut his losses and said:

"I think we are getting away from the object of the visit. Neither my boss has come to ask how he organizes his band, nor to explain how he organizes his. It was convenient that we all get to know each other to avoid any unnecessary stumbling and that's it. You already know me and I know you, the rest strike.

"Right, and these around me are some of my men. The others are scattered around and I cannot pick them up to make the presentation, but they already know something about him and time will have to be known.

"Well, in that case, for my part I have nothing to do here. If my boss wants to stay, let him do it.

Foot, after a moment's hesitation, replied:

"No, Stuart; I came just to please you. We agreed on a delimitation of places and since then we have refrained from meddling in opposing fiefdoms. I do not want this to serve as a precedent.

"You're sorry, Foot," Fritt stated. I realize the reason for the visit and I appreciate it. Anyway, if I can be of use to you ...

"Thanks; I think we can both get along very well without outside help.

"At least, so far, we've proven it," Fritt said.

They shook hands and Foot, with his second, left the southern part. Stuart was annoyed by the insinuations of his rival, because they could ignite the doubt in the mind of Foot. Furious, he commented:

"I don't like that guy. He is foolish and ignorant. I did not think that being anything more than a shooting machine was an inconvenience. I'd like to see your guys in a hurry to see what they figured out. When he wanted to step in and think, he might have none left.

"It is possible, but he has been lucky and achieved something of what he set out to do. I couldn't catch him in time.

"That has stung my self-esteem, boss. I would like to answer with your own weapons and I will study it. Would you really like to sweep him up and be alone?

"You don't even wonder, Stuart.

"Well, don't betThere was nothing for the life of Fritt.

"Watch out. Killing him would solve nothing.

"Who says no? He has confessed that he only has arms and not heads. That being the case, who was going to effectively take over the band? With a little ingenuity, they would all be swept away. Not that I think it's easy, but I promise to study it.

"Well, do it, but you will end up convincing yourself that it would be like sitting on top of a porcupine. I am not soft or give up easily, and yet I chose to do this arrangement and it is best left at that.

"However you want; I'm not very keen, although I could use a doubling of income.

Stuart left Foot in his lair and withdrew. It was two o'clock and Agnes's den was still in full swing, but he was not tempted to return to it. He guessed that doing so would make his life more difficult and he preferred to try to cool it down.

Agnes had awakened very late to the hurricane of passions and this was very dangerous for a woman like her. He had to pour cold water on the fire so it wouldn't explode, at least as long as he wasn't free from Foot and became the master of the situation. Then he wouldn't mind facing her, because his teeth would be chipped and he couldn't cause any dangerous bites.

CHAPTER IX

THE FIERCE FEELS JEALOUS

I know introduced Stuart the next night at the joint. Agnes, who was suffering from a severe headache that night "perhaps a product of the concerns that Stuart's somewhat strange behavior was causing her," had retired to her rooms, lying on the bed for a while to try to get that annoyance over.

Stuart was glad Agnes was gone. If she was absent, he could always justify that he had gone to see her, and that, although the logical thing was to be interested in her condition, the prudence of not being suspicious of her attentions had prevented him from going up to see her.

This served as a pretext for him to be extremely attentive to Betty. The girl, although a little fearful, could not resist against the attraction that Stuart exerted on her, and ignoring Agnes's warnings she dedicated all her free time to him and danced with him without worrying about the rest of the customers, who felt mortified by that preference of the young woman.

But despite this, Stuart found her shy and fearful, and trying to find out what was wrong with her, he asked:

"What's the matter with you, girl? It seems that you are not very comfortable with me.

"Why not? I feel very good.

"However, I notice you are somewhat scared. Has someone said anything bad about me?

The young woman, after a moment's hesitation, replied:

"Well ... up to a point. It wasn't exactly bad at all, but Agnes ...

He felt revolted when he realized that it was something of "the Californian Beauty" and bellowed:

"What did that smug birria tell you?

"For God's sake, don't yell like that. If it came to her ears, it would be terrible. He has warned me that his business is above all else and that I owe my work to him. I don't want her to spend my time with anyone in particular, and from her point of view I can't blame her, but sometimes I wonder if she will feel jealous for no reason.

Stuart smiled in amusement when he realized that Betty had inadvertently hit the mark.

Jealous of what? "I ask.

"Because of your preference for me. Of course that's silly, because her attention to me is normal and because I don't think Agnes is capable of fixing her eyes on any man.

"And why do you listen to him? You will always have an audience that admires and pampers you. I was the first and ...

"Thank you, but I have to take care of my job, because nowhere would I be better than here. Agnes considers me and ... there is no owner who overwhelms me and tries to impose certain conditions on me ...

"That you would not admit.

"That I wouldn't admit... unless I was cornered. That is why I have to watch what I do, even if I feel it.

"Hasn't a man come across you who decides to withdraw you from this cage?

"I would be lying if I said no. There were some who suggested it to me, but did that solve anything?

"Live quietly, without being forced to endure certain things.

"And sometimes, having to put up with worse ones. There are men who neither for what they can offer nor for what they can actually give can be tolerated.

"What kind of man is he that you like?

"You want us not to talk about it? All women are ambitious and I am no exception, but sometimes ambitions meet insurmountable barriers and my moral situation does not allow me ...

He, in an impulsive outburst of the many he used to have, said without thinking:

"Hang on a bit, Betty. One day I will be the master of San Francisco, and that day ... you will be the master with me. I like you for many things that I would not be able to explain, and I am also ambitious when it comes to women.

Betty blushed and he held her against his chest. They danced without realizing their surroundings, until, as they faced the steps, Stuart raised his head and discovered Agnes, leaning against the verandah, gazing at them with concentrated attention. In the gleam of the "Californian Beauty" eyes he read all the anger and resentment that the contemplation was producing in him.

But determined to face the situation with the impetus that characterized him, he ignored it. He was not a man capable of being subjugated by a woman and he would have the most boisterous argument with her, but he would make no show of being afraid of her.

But Betty saw it too, and losing her color stuttered awkwardly:

"Excuse me for leaving you. There is Agnes and I suspect she has been bothered by me dancing with me.

"Ignore it, and if he says something to you later, apologize to me. Someday we will give him a serious upset.

But the music had ended and Betty took the opportunity to separate from him and meet other clients. Agnes then began to descend and with a gesture called Stuart to her side.

The latter, unconcerned, approached saying:

"I asked about you and they told me that your head hurt a little and you had gone to bed. It seems that your headache has passed and I celebrate it. Or are you not better?

"Enough to see how little you care about me despite your promises.

"You are absurd, Agnes" he affirmed while filling the glasses ". I have already told you that I came to see you and when I asked about you they gave me that warning. It shouldn't increase your headache and even less show off your favorite by going up to your private rooms in full view of everyone.

"Do not apologize. You're already bothering me with so much secrecy that I can't understand. I do what I want and so do you. If sooner or later it is to be known, I don't know why those prudish things of yours.

"I've already given you a reason. I don't want complications with Foot for now. He is in love with you and endures his momentum because he believes that there is no one involved. If he knew that it was precisely me who stood in the way of his aspirations, the mess would be great.

"All of these are pretexts. What interests you is the freedom to be distracted with all of them, and especially with some especially.

"That is your bullshit. I've danced with several in the short time I've been here. You don't have to think about things that you only imagine.

"Well, we'll clear that up. I have lived a long time to know how to appreciate certain things, and I know that men are so absurd that you value what they don't give you and despise what they put at hand.

"Do you want to shut up now, princess? The headache makes you see visions. Sit down and drink to see if that passes you by.

"It won't go away. I just want to warn you of one thing, and that is that I am a special woman for everything. You will have me by your side whenever you need it as long as you correspond loyally, but if it were not so ... no enemy more fierce and worse for you than me.

Stuart guessed that she wasn't fooling him and that it would work out, but he was counting on her audacity and skill to do the least harm in the worst case scenario.

"Tell me about something less sour, sweetie. I came just to see you and you are making me bitter at the moment. Why?

"No reason; I've already given you my reasons. Are you coming to stay tonight?

He decided to calm his anger for the moment and replied:

"If you want it, I'll stay.

"That seems like a more positive proof of affection to me. It was about time you had some time to dedicate it to me.

"You well know how busy I've been with Foot these days. Fortunately, things are normalizing.

"Well, I appreciate the trait, but I don't want to make your night bitter. I am not feeling well and I need to rest. Does it seem better to you tomorrow if I find myself answered?

He saw the open sky with the reply and replied:

"Whatever you send, sweetie. I am your slave.

"What you are is a fresco without salvation. We agree that tomorrow, but you are going to do the favor of leaving right now so that you solve what you have to solve and tomorrow you dedicate all your time to me. I'll invite you to dinner at ten. You go up through the side door and I will leave everything ready so that no one interrupts us.

"Very good. At ten you will have me here.

He got up ready to leave, because the offer had been forced and he felt more at home away from Agnes's tyrannical influence. The next day he would invent a pretext for not going to dinner, and what would result from the sit-in would already be seen.

Agnes followed him with her eyes until she saw him disappear, then smiled with savage humor. She was ready to cut all competition attempts, and the next day she was going to surprise her. Depending on how he reacted to her, he could gauge the kind of interest he felt for her person.

He did not retreat to his rooms as promised. It was a studied plan to drive Stuart away and maneuver as he had intended. She stayed in the living room until closing time, and when it was almost empty and the girls were about to leave, she called Betty and said:

"Before you go go up to my rooms. I have to talk to you.

The girl stiffened. Something instinctive told her that things had gotten complicated and that she was going to be the victim of Agnes's bad mood.

He collected his clothes and went up to the private rooms of the owner of the gambling den. She was waiting for her in the cabinet.

"Something happens? Betty asked.

"Yes, my dear, something happens, and God knows I'm sorry, but things have to be this way. I gave you a friendly warning because she appreciated you for what you are worth and you have disdained her. I thought that knowing me as you know me better than your peers would take my advice into consideration.

"I don't know what you mean," replied the young woman, although from the first moment she knew from which side of the wound she was breathing.

"You know it, and you are a hypocrite denying it. You like that stranger you became very fond of very early on, and that hurts me in the extreme. As I do not admit any man is given preference in my establishment and you persist in doing so, I have decided to do without your services despite not being ignorant of your worth. I am going to make your account and I am sure that it will not take long to find another place to provide your services.

The girl was hurt by such a sharp decision and replied:

"You have no reason to do that. Stuart is a client like any other and I have served him like others. You seem to forget that many nights, when a good customer has spent many dollars on drinks through me, you have been the first to advise me to dedicate myself to him and not to leave his hand.

"Does Stuart spend a lot? Agnes said wryly.

"Do not look selfishly at money" was the reply.

"The eyes with which you look at him make you see him that way," said Agnes incisively, "and that is precisely what compels me to make this determination. You like Stuart too much, and that and not the desire to serve me is what guides you to dedicate your preferences to him. You have become infatuated with him and it is what I do not tolerate.

Betty, stung, stirred saying:

"Why? Because you like it too?

"If so, what does it matter to you?

"Of course I care," replied the girl bravely. From employee to owner I cannot compete with you, but from woman to woman I can.

Agnes bristled. He could admit anything unless anyone challenged him on that ground.

"From woman to woman you say? Are you forgetting that I have had half the men of San Francisco at my feet and have despised them all?

Betty, without any contemplation towards her, affirmed:

"Well, that must have been because they all had their knees too soft to bend in their wake. You may be the owner of this joint and wear many jewels, but forget that there are men who are not interested in any of that and instead I am twenty years younger than you.

Those phrases were like a string of daggers aimed squarely at the heart of "Californian Beauty." Betty had called her old and she couldn't tolerate it.

"Twenty years younger? What do you know my age? But, even if it were, I have plenty of what you lack to entangle a man if it is my taste: world and wisdom.

"And do you think that in this case that will help you?

"We'll see. If you intend to challenge me, I will tell you that Stuart will only be for me, and that I will roll him like a ball in front of me.

"I summon you to get it," replied the girl, glaring at her.

"We'll see, Betty, and I'm going to tell you something else. I'm going to give you your salary and an order. Get out of San Francisco and don't try to overshadow me there. Do not forget that my power here is great and that if I considered you a hindrance you would live very little to laugh at it. It is something that I warn you because I do not want to be cruel to you.

"I will not get out of here" she affirmed energetically ". You can fire me, but I won't lack a place to work, or men to protect me.

"Not being Stuart, the others matter little to me.

"It will be the one I want and choose. I don't have to tell you about that.

"We will see that, and do not dream of acting on this side, where Foot is the owner. I would give whatever I asked, even if I had to surrender to him to do so, and you know how I spend it when I get angry. If you think I'm going to allow you to stay so that Stuart is in a position to visit you freely, you're wrong. Go to the south side, where he is forbidden to look out safely, and that he does not know more about you.

"I'll go where I want or can, and if Stuart has a penchant for me, he's a man who can't be stopped by anything. This is my last word.

"He will not do it, because before he would shoot him down.

He threw several gold coins on the table, saying:

"There you have what I owe you. Pick up all of yours and get out, but don't forget my threats. I've become infatuated with Stuart and as long as I don't tire of him and dismiss him as useless, I'm not giving him up to anyone.

Betty, transfigured, did not want to further sour the discussion, but intimately promised not to give in to her rival. She was challenging her vanity and self-esteem as a woman, and she was determined to accept it with all its consequences.

He put the money away and went downstairs to collect his work clothes. As she emerged out onto the deserted, dark road, she was tempted to head over to Stuart's lodge to give him an account of what had happened, but common sense told her that the time was not very conducive to going to the inn. He would wait until it was daylight and visit him giving him a background on the causes of his dismissal.

She wasn't quite sure that Stuart had any fondness for Agnes, and if he checked it out, what happened next would show.

And without being able to control his rage, he retired to his lodging.

* * *

It was about one o'clock and Stuart was about to leave his bed when one of the waiters went up to his apartment to warn him that a very attractive young woman was asking for him.

Stuart almost guessed who it was. The night before he had not left the gambling den very convinced of Agnes's resignation and he feared that in his vanity and jealousy he had retaliated against Betty.

"Didn't you give your name? He asked the waiter.

"No, sir" he just said that he needed to speak to you urgently.

"Well, ask her if her name is Betty, and if she says yes, have them make breakfast for two. I am coming right away.

He dressed and washed carefully, and half an hour later he appeared in the dining room, still deserted. The waiter was preparing a table with two cutlery.

Betty was waiting for him standing by a table. He advanced towards her with outstretched hands and a cheerful smile on his friendly face.

"How are you here, girl? "He said taking her by the arm." They couldn't wake me up in a more pleasant way. Come and sit here, I invite you to lunch and then you will tell me the reason for this pleasant visit.

She was flattered by the deference, but unable to control her uneasiness, she said as she sat down:

"It was not coming to this. I came to tell you that Agnes fired me from the joint last night.

He looked at her, and always smiling, he replied:

"I had guessed it when your visit was announced. On what has that parrot been founded to do such a thing?

"In that she is jealous of me" affirmed Betty categorically.

"Well, in her position I would feel like her. There is something that does not give the position or the money, and that Agnes cannot get it.

"He made me say something similar to him, and he went through the roof. He has declared that he is not willing to admit competitions and has threatened me.

"What threatened you, you say?

"Yes. He has ordered me to leave San Francisco if I do not want to expose myself to serious danger. He says not to apply for a job in any premises that Foot controls, because I would ask him to suppress me, even if I had to give in to him. He wants to avoid by all means that you see me; And as for you, you have said that you would shoot her down if she did not succeed in surrendering to her whim.

"Well, that's going to be a bit difficult for him," Stuart said resolutely.

She after a moment's hesitation, asked:

"Tell me the truth, Stuart. What is there between you and her to make you so fiercely jealous?

"Well ... nothing that she would like, and this is what makes her angry. He has made a silly illusion that I have not wanted to vanish, because at the moment it does not suit me, but if he persists, things will get right no matter what happens. You are taking it too seriously and I do not consent to it.

"Watch out. He will have to walk with leaden feet, because he will take advantage of his influence with Foot to take him on with all his men. He knows what he would give for her to make him face and is capable of doing it in order to emerge triumphant.

Stuart pondered. He knew what Betty was implying was true and now he regretted certain confidences he had made to Agnes. If she gave Foot an account of her plans to become the owner of San Francisco, the gunman would not hesitate to try to sweep her away.

Without losing his cool, he assured:

"Don't worry, girl, everything will be fine. What are you planning to do now?

"I do not know. I am disoriented.

"Well, I'm going to tell you. You are going to leave your lodging and you are going to come to live in this same inn. You will not apply for a job anywhere and you will wait.

"I need to work. Here the money runs out soon.

"I earn more than I need. You will not need to spend anything and you will wait for the situation to be clarified. It can't be long because this is a powder keg with a lit fuse. It has to explode from one moment to another and we will see who it reaches.

"What are you planning to do?

"Nothing on my part. I'll force them to blow it up and we'll see how far the hole goes. After the smoke clears I will know how to act.

"Be very careful with Agnes. I know her and I know that she will not hesitate to put her life in danger.

"I will take care of me for the account you have for me. You eat and don't worry. Today I don't have much to do and I will dedicate the day to you. Tonight we will know if something is going to happen.

He didn't want to talk about it any more, and when lunch was over he had the best available room ready for Betty. Then he left it on her, saying:

Don't be startled or worried. I don't know what time I'll be back tonight or if I'll be back, but trust me. I am a high-flying eagle so that no one can lower me in the dark.

* * *

Agnes had a feverish day. He had given in to a violent outburst of jealousy by firing Betty, but he wondered what the consequences were going to be. He was beginning to gauge Stuart's character and was afraid that Stuart's reaction would backfire. Perhaps he would have gained more by not giving so many flights to the matter, but if he felt challenged, it would be the revelation of the truth and the initiation of a terrible duel between the two.

He waited feverishly for the appointment time. He had ordered a great menu to be made and it had been retouched like never before.

But at ten o'clock, the castle of illusions that he had built fell apart with a letter that was delivered to him. It was from Stuart and it said simply, "Don't wait for me for dinner tonight because I won't be there."

The letter said no more, but it was enough. He must have learned of Betty's dismissal and its causes, and with the harshness and abruptness that he knew how to use in everything, he replied with that contempt. His anger was such that in a fit of hysteria he kicked the table and threw it on the floor with all the precious dishes.

Glasses and plates collided with an infernal crash as they broke, and the black woman who served him came terrified, but Agnes, throwing a piece of glass at his head, roared:

"Go away, you filthy rat! I do not want to see anybody!

The servant girl withdrew in fright and Agnes vented her anger by kicking the fragments of the tableware. Then, her face fading from tears as she ran, over her makeup, she retired to her bedroom and dropped to the bed, hyperarously desperate.

CHAPTER X

STUART PLAYS HIS EXTENSIONS

With his nerves alert, Stuart let the day go by waiting for the night, those nights that he loved so much because for his temperament the empire of the shadows was his own empire, could bring him. Until it was time for her appointment with Agnes, she knew that no one was going to happen, and then ... her bad or good luck would mark the end of this dramatic adventure.

Therefore, at ten o'clock he decided to meet with Foot and not part with him if possible. As a pretext, he would use certain embryonic ideas he had to attack Fritt, and surely the discussion would have them together for a good part of the night.

He was not wrong. The gunman listened to him with interest and began to discuss his ideas with him one by one, exposing the inconveniences he found for their realization. Stuart knew them in advance, but his goal was not to be separated from Foot all night. Until at twelve they brought him a letter. Foot opened it strangely, and when he learned of the brief content, he said:

"Let's save this discussion for another more suitable time, Stuart. Agnes begs me to go urgently, as something must happen to her for this call at such times.

"Bah! "Stuart said disparagingly, although he could not hide the effect he felt at the abrupt reaction of the angry woman." Maybe she remembers that she lives alone and longs for her company

"Agnes? "Foot replied, incredulous." You don't know her well. She is a marble woman, and no matter how hard I have tried to conquer her, I have always failed.

Don't despair. Sometimes things are achieved when they are least expected, and this I know from experience. I would go hopeful instead, because one day, maybe tonight, you need something extraordinary from you and then compensation is imposed.

"I don't believe in any of that.

"I do, because I have hunches. Just in case, be prepared. A woman who calls a man urgently at this hour is not on a whim, and if the thing is worth it, it will always be worthy of being taken into account. Good luck to you.

Foot started to leave. Before he asked:

"Are you accompanying me?

"For what? I don't think I'm gallant, because those things are private and I don't like to disturb idylls.

"So what will you do?

"I'm going to El Ace de Corazón.

"It's okay. If I need you, I'll look for you there.

They parted ways, and Foot, quite intrigued by this unexpected call, headed for Agnes's den. When he entered the premises, everything was in order. A large audience, a lot of animation and nothing that denounced a lack of normality.

One of the guardians of the premises, upon seeing him, indicated:

"They await you upstairs, Mr. Foot.

He hurried up the stairs and reached the rooms of "Californian Beauty."

When he entered the receiving room, nothing denounced the violent fury of the scene. The damage had disappeared, the floor was clean and the coffee water was boiling on the table. The box with the cigars and whiskey was not missing either.

Agnes, the tragic traces of her anger erased, appeared as always with makeup. Lying in an indolent attitude, she was smoking a cigarette and smiling with attraction. Foot greeted her with a bow of his head and then gallantly kissed her soft hand, She indicated a seat, saying:

"Sit here next to me, Foot. I hope you are not in a great hurry because we have to talk.

Foot remembered Stuart's insinuations and winced. It seemed as if a telepathic current had encouraged him to speak and the consequences were about to arrive for him.

Anxiously, he replied:

"I sit where you order and I do what you ask me to do. You always know it and I don't need to repeat it to you, but to show it to you when you need it.

"I know, and don't think I haven't thought about it many times. I always had a strong suspicion with men in general, but when one is constant, knows how to wait and reaches degrees that others did not know or did not want to reach, he deserves to be noticed.

"Don't make me hopeful, Agnes," said the gunman nervously. Understand how unpleasant it would be for me to lose you afterward.

"Who knows. We all have at our fingertips things that sometimes seem impossible. It could be that your time has come.

"About what?

"To get what you want.

"Don't play with me on that ground, Agnes" said Foot getting up from the seat and planting himself in front of her to stare into her eyes. " It would be a very dangerous game. Why did you send for me?

Agnes, without abandoning her smiling attitude, replied:

"I like you, Foot, I like you more every day because you are a stubborn, whole and tough man. As I like men. I just wonder if you would be as affectionate to a woman as you would be rough with those of your gender.

"Have you ever tried to test it? I have given you the opportunity to do so and you rejected it.

"It's true, but I think I'm going to put you to the test, Foot. You want to give me a kiss?

He looked at her puzzled and approached. It was she who kissed him and then, rejecting him, said when she stood up abruptly:

"This may be a foretaste of a lot, but you have to earn it. I'm sure you will.

How am I to do it? He asked frantically.

"Killing a man.

"I have killed so many, that if it deserved an award of such caliber, I would have the women hanging around my neck by the dozen. If your love only costs the life of one more man, I can offer you the life of five or six as compensation.

"Just one is enough for me, Foot.

"Well, tell me who he is and how you want me to kill him, if in your presence, with gunshots, or with bits.

"Killing him, I don't care how you do it. This is your second, Stuart.

"What do you say? Asked Foot in amazement.

"It is him and I will give you several reasons to justify wanting his death. Stuart is a vain and conceited man who believes that he can achieve anything when he wants it, and one of the things he tries to achieve ... is me, but his vanity is so great, that he has exceeded himself. To try to conquer me, forgetting or despising that you and I are true friends, and also forgetting that you are in love with me, because he knows it, he has made me offers that demonstrate his cynicism.

"He has told me that if I listen to him and agree to his wishes, he will remove you from the world, because he has studied the way to eliminate you and take over your crew. As soon as I say yes to him, he has promised to kill you before you know it and take over your fiefdom. He offered me a share of the profits and even dreams of later eliminating Fritt and being the absolute owner of San Francisco.

»I listened to him trying to suppress my indignation and my rage. I did not want to put him on his guard with a refusal and a rejection, and to gain time I answered that I would think about it and tomorrow night I would give him a definitive answer, but in fear that he would go ahead, more if I was suspicious that he might warn you of the danger you are running, that is why I hastened to send you a message for you to come tonight. We had that conversation very recently and I was quick to put my guard on my guard as was my duty as a friend.

Foot, who had heard Agnes's fallacious words pale with anger, gnashed his teeth in an impressive way and bellowed:

"That this guy feels capable of eliminating me?

"That has been his proposition. I felt so humiliated by her when I realized that she wanted to buy me with the price of your life, that I couldn't help but react. You can get me with my own weapons to convince women, but not by valuing me that way. Between you who have offered me so much without grievances and he who offers me the impossible at the cost of betrayal, I have not doubted. I prefer you and when you have eliminated that vulture, I will know how to deliver as you deserve.

"You really will, Agnes? Asked Foot, nervous with enthusiasm.

"When you know that Stuart is dead, come ask me" she replied offering him the best of her smiles.

"Stuart will die tonight. I know where I can find him now and I promise to bring his body right here to convince you. Wait just long for me to find him and fulfill my promise.

He strode toward the exit door to the reserved ladder and yanked the latch out, but a voice metallic and wounding like a knife and the cold barrel of a revolver threatening his chest held him back.

"Not yet, Foot, that is still too early. Before I allow you to try, you have to listen to me and you too, Agnes. Be very careful not to make the slightest movement while I speak, or you will not finish listening to my story.

She and he froze in amazement and fear at being threatened by the adventurer's revolver. The least they could have suspected was having him so close to them, when Foot believed him calmly drinking at the Ace of Heart.

But Stuart was audacious. After leaving Foot, he followed him until he saw him enter the joint, and later, from the revolving door, saw him go up to the gallery. He guessed what was going to happen and devised a daring plan. If he could climb the reserved stairway without being seen, he might be surprised at what they were talking about and he would know how to proceed next.

And luck favored him. The maid had been led away by Agnes with an order not to interrupt them, and the corridor was deserted.

Close to the door, he listened to the entire conversation and felt anger at Agnes's double-down. Brazenly lying to him, he had told her only the truth that it was only in her best interest to incite him to kill him.

Without ceasing to dominate them with the weapon, he exclaimed:

"Now it's my turn to speak up, Foot, and tell you what she has kept quiet about. It might not do you any good to know, but just in case. If there is any woman in the world who is selfish and worthy of contempt, it is Agnes. All his life he has played, according to his own confession, with men, without mercy or love towards anyone and you have not been an exception in the game.

"Perhaps she did it out of the vanity of humiliating those who begged her so much, but that's the way it was, and only a man who neither flattered her nor asked for anything achieved what the others did not, and that was me. But it has taken things too far. Whoever asks for nothing is not obliged to give anything and she has wanted everything from me. Her passion for any concept did not suit me and I wanted to leave that dangerous bud dead before it grew, but she tried to rivet it and make it eternal.

»I am too young to digest steaks that have been soggy from the years at ease and she has not wanted to understand it. In his jealousy, he has victimized someone who had nothing to do with this matter and has fired Betty from the premises, just because she danced at ease with me and I with her. He even threatened to force you to kill her if she did not disappear from San Francisco, as if with that unworthy death she could keep me by her side.

"Tonight he had asked me to have dinner at ten o'clock. I sent her two letters telling her that I would not come, and in her spite and rage she took you as an instrument of her revenge. For those who lack all scruples, the payment did not matter to them and that is why they called you.

I was expecting this reaction. That's why I tried not to part with you tonight and when you received the letter, I guessed what you were called for. Remember that I warned you that perhaps your love aspirations would be fulfilled when you least expected. But since I am not willing to give you the advantage of using your men to harass me like a rabid cat, I have decided to leave things to their normal proportions. From you to me, from man to man, everything is fine, but with advantages for you, no.

"She has not meditated that her selfishness could be the cause of your death and not mine. Now he will convince himself that he has made a mistake again, because he will. You have promised to bring my corpse here to give him that satisfaction; I will leave him yours so that his anger and despair are even greater. I have been able to wait for you and finish you with impunity. I can also do it here with both of you. Just pleasing the finger would suffice, but I am a little more noble than all that and I am going to offer you a minimal chance of success.

Suddenly, before Foot had time to follow the movement, he holstered his revolver, commanding in a metallic voice:

"Quick draw, Foot.

The gunman did not make himself repeat the order and pulled the handle of his colt. Stuart drew again as fast as he had stowed the revolver, and two shots vibrated before his enemy had time to fire at him. Foot, hit in the chest at such close range, leaned heavily to one side and fell on Agnes, who with a hallucinatory howl of horror and rage pushed him away, fleeing to her bedroom, perhaps fearing that Stuart would do the same to her. she.

But Stuart didn't care about her. He was not a man capable of killing a woman, though like that he would have laid such a cowardly trap for him. Knowing that the explosion would have caused the alarm in the room, he hastened to gain the ladder and to lose himself in the shadows of the night, those gloomy and mysterious shadows in which death came round and which could be more easily outwitted than in full sun.

He hurriedly left the great avenue and lost himself through various alleys to erase his trail. Now he knew he was in a very precarious situation, because although he had suppressed Foot, as was his idea, he had been forced to hasten his plans and that was not the way to eliminate him to have the support of his men.

Now they would seek him like wolves to finish him off and he needed to do something without wasting time. He could take advantage of those same shadows and flee, but this was something that did not fit his temperament. He only fled when the situation got desperate and it wasn't yet. As long as he was free to move, he was still a dangerous enemy. This would have to be verified by others to give it all the value it possessed.

What in many moments he was going to do, he did not know, but if he did not seek a solution during the reign of the shadows, he would not achieve it in the clear light of the sun.

Suddenly he devised a daring plan. Something of boundless audacity and danger that might or might not work, but if it turned out as he was projecting it, he might gain more from it than he could lose.

And quickly, retracing the path, he reached the part of the street where Fritt had his fiefdom. Perhaps they would not look for him there for fear of complications, and if he was lucky enough to run into Fritt soon, he might emerge triumphant from the rugged challenge.

In this part of the avenue, everything was calm and quiet, which seemed to indicate that word had not yet spread of Foot's death.

When he reached the joint where his short-lived boss's rival used to stay for a few hours at night, he peeked inside through the revolving half-door entrance. The step he was about to take was too risky in itself and he could not forget the gunman's misgivings of him and how he had expressed himself about the future.

But he had no other solution. Ally with him to get the best possible advantage for the time being or risk being hunted on any street corner by the very men of his gang who would not forgive him for the death of their boss.

He discovered Fritt sitting at a table playing poker with three others. It didn't seem like the right time to approach him by interrupting the game, but he had no choice but to do so.

He pushed open the door and entered. Fritt turned his head quickly and when he discovered him, he took a deep look at him and seemed intrigued by his presence.

As Stuart approached the table decisively, the gunman turned slightly in his seat to face him and looked at him questioningly.

"Good night, Stuart," he said. How you around here?

"I'd like to speak with you for a few minutes, Fritt. It's something that I think may interest you.

"I hear you, Stuart.

"I'm sorry, but it is of a particular nature. Later, if you deem it necessary to make what we talk known, I will not oppose it.

Fritt calmly collected his money, putting down the cards. Then he pointed to a door at the back, indicating:

"Follow me.

One of their table companions got up ready to follow them. Fritt stopped him coldly, saying:

"Needless.

But Stuart offered Fritt:

"If you need me to hand over my revolver as a guarantee that I am only here to speak with you, I will hand it over, but at the moment I do not want anyone to intervene in our conversation.

He raised his arms showing the holster to be disarmed. Fritt replied:

"It is not precise, Frank, retreat.

The bodyguard obeyed and they both entered a dark corridor lit by a swinging oil lamp, until they reached a booth.

Already in it, Fritt indicated a seat:

Sit down and talk. All of this seems very mysterious to me, Stuart, but I suppose there is some compelling reason for this interview.

Yes, a bit mysterious indeed, and that reason exists, but you are the one who must decide whether it should be trumpeted or whether it should remain a secret. Do you want to honestly answer a question?

"If there is no reason to oblige me otherwise, I will gladly do so. I asked for.

"Would you like to be the absolute owner of the street of San Francisco?

Fritt looked at him intently, replying:

"That would please me as Foot would, but I don't think it's in their power to grant it to any of us.

"Maybe that's where I'm wrong. It is something that I am in a position to offer you at this time.

Fritt coldly replied:

"If you have taken me for a fool to strike dangerous hooks, you have taken the wrong measure ... and that can be very dangerous for you.

"There is no bait, but a reality that you can calibrate whenever you want. If you are interested, I am in a position to offer you what you longed for so much and what you had to give up because you could not with such a hard bite as it was to eliminate Foot from your step.

"What price do you intend to put on his betrayal? Fritt asked dismissively.

"Price, none, because there is no betrayal, but then I leave it to your judgment to just appreciate what I offer you. I want to warn with rude sincerity that I am making the offer to you because you are in a position to take the fruit and I am not; if it were, on the contrary, I would have kept it for myself.

"And what is it about?

"I just killed Foot.

Fritt vibrated like a steel spring. Then, repeating his inquisitorial gaze, he asked:

"Why did you just kill Foot?

"I have said that 'I have killed Foot' not that I have murdered him and I can prove that I killed him man to man and giving him time to draw. I was not in my mind to do so, but fate arranged it that way and I had to fight the matter.

And if that has been the case, why not take advantage of the occasion?

"I've already told you because I can't. It is not generosity, but necessity, and before the fruit of that death is lost, I offer it to whoever can collect it. It is the self-preservation instinct and the pride of not disappearing like a coward that brings me here. I killed Foot for something that had nothing to do with the business and without me looking for a fight. It was all born out of the jealousy of the most despicable of women, and since I was urging her to kill me, I had to get ahead of myself.

"Agnes, perhaps? Asked Fritt, intrigued.

"Yes. She tried to catch me in her networks and because I despised her she called Foot telling her lies and asking him to kill me in exchange for ... agreeing to be her friend when she had despised her so many times. He, who was still infatuated with her, promised to bring her my corpse in exchange for that promise. There was no option and before he killed me I killed him, but I did it face to face, in front of her and giving her time to draw.

"Tell me what happened.

Stuart gave him a cursory account of the event. Then he added:

"After all this, what could I do? I would have to fight alone with the rest of the crew and I am not a colossus nor can I be in twenty places at once. They will look for me to eliminate me and as someone has to take advantage of that death, no one better than you, who is organized and can fight them in these moments of disorientation before they rebuild and name someone to replace Foot. With his rival dead, the only solid head to take the reins was me and it is not time. When they see smoothies and without a boss, they will be able to do nothing and you will be the absolute master of the street.

"And you, what will it be?

"I leave it up to you. Maybe later it can be useful to you, believe it or not.

Fritt, after thinking for a moment, replied:

"Wait for me here a bit.

She went out into the hall and called Frank, talking to him in a low voice for a few minutes. His second quickly left the tavern.

Fritt returned to the booth and facing the adventurer said coldly:

"Listen, Stuart, I appreciate knowing men and I thought I knew you as soon as I saw you. You are not one to be a lion tail if you think you can be a mouse head.

"Not even that," Stuart boldly replied, "or lion head, or nothing."

"I am glad that he is so sincere. You can be a very useful man, but as dangerous as sitting on a powder keg with the fuse burning. This is why I would never admit him to my gang.

"What am i going to do! I will resign myself.

"But I don't want to take advantage of your work and your offer either, because if I did, I would still have you as an enemy and I would be forced to eliminate you, or at least to try. That is why I make you a good proposition.

"Come on.

"I am going to try what you propose to me as soon as the news and reports that I have ordered are brought to me. You will help me clear the street of enemies to ensure success and when this is consolidated, I will give you ten thousand dollars as payment for your services and you will ride a horse and leave San Francisco forever.

"He assures me that he has fallen in love with that girl named Betty and that he has her in his custody. With that money he can take her away and find a quieter place for the two of them to settle by his side, start a new campaign, far from here, or dedicate himself to caring for the land as a well-deserved break from his activities. If he accepts it, we will both have come out winning with the pact.

Stuart didn't hesitate for a moment:

"Okay," he replied, "I only impose one condition.

Say it.

"Let me settle our differences with Agnes after everything is over.

"Would I be able to kill her? Fritt asked.

"Do not. I am not a murderer of women, if Agnes can be called a woman, but somehow I have to punish her betrayal and her lies. She has gained a lot at the cost of exposing little and wears very expensive jewelry on her hands and neck. I think Betty's neck and hands will look better.

"Good. That doesn't matter to me. For you Agnes and her damn jewels. What I want is the other.

"Then no more talk. From this moment he has me at his command.

Let's wait for Frank to come back and confirm his news. Then we will do the cleaning. Come with me.

They went out into the living room. Fritt ordered that the absent members of his gang be urgently searched by all the premises of his jurisdiction and that they should gather there as quickly as possible. The night was going to be tragic and hectic and it needed all its elements. As they arrived he ordered a bottle of whiskey to be served and offered Stuart a drink; it provided:

"By the sole owner of San Francisco.

"Because you see it before you leave it.

And they both drained their glasses looking into each other's eyes intensely.

CHAPTER XI

THE TRAGIC NIGHT

A little later Frank returned. There was a certain nervousness in his face, and with a nod he nodded to what Fritt was asking him with his eyes.

"What's over there?

"A big stir, boss. I've been able to observe that Agnes's joint is abuzz with people. Even at the door the curious crowd.

Have you seen someone you know?

"Yes. I saw Walter "the Cross-eyed", James "the Ferret" and Jim "Six Fingers." Inside there must be some more.

"Good. As soon as our men gather, prepare yourselves with lead. We are going to intervene in the party.

Frank and the other two who were playing with Fritt when Stuart came in gave their boss a puzzled look.

"We? Is there something there that affects us? Said one.

"Much. We are going to take advantage of the event to achieve what until now we had not achieved. Dead Foot, who was the organizing head, they lack a boss and before they organize themselves, we are going to take advantage of the confusion. When the sun comes up, we have to be the sole owners of San Francisco.

"Does that mean there will be a fight again?

"Whatever they want to accept. When we catch them by surprise and clear their ranks, they will be convinced that they have nothing to do here anymore. Get ready.

Little by little, men began to arrive. Tough and ill-faced guys, men already hardened in the ups and downs of the fight, who came intrigued by the call and who glanced at Stuart, wondering who this guy was and what they wanted from them.

Fritt, cold and dominating, was explaining in broad strokes what happened and what he needed from them. They were going to take a rampage down the street of San Francisco and ruthlessly remove every obstacle that would oppose what they longed for so much and for which they had fought so much before.

A quarter of an hour later, Fritt had gathered twenty men around him. When he counted them, he missed a couple of them, but he wasn't about to wait any longer. All the time that was lost, she could work against him and she didn't want it to happen that way.

Gesturing to Stuart, he ordered:

"Go. You by my side.

"Wherever you want. I will not turn my face at the time of the celebration.

Fritt did not reply and Stuart asked a question:

"Do you already have a plan of attack?

"Not much but some. If most of them are in Agnes's joint, I think that's where we should start.

"I think so too. When word has spread, they will have come to be convinced that Foot's death is true. There you can make a good raid.

On the road, Fritt gave sharp orders. All had to be divided into two small groups and by different paths flow in front of the gambling den in a given minute.

"It's two o'clock," he said, consulting his watch. At a quarter past two, everyone in front of the door.

They parted, lost in the shadows of the night. As the gang slipped through the affluent streets, Fritt was left with Stuart, Frank, and another gunman.

At a slow pace, timing so as not to be ahead or behind, they moved up the street. The lights of the establishments were outlined in quadrilaterals on the dust of the road, and from the interiors came the murmur of the happy voices of the customers.

All that part was still calm. The word had not spread and this satisfied Fritt. When the first detonations vibrated, it would be time for the alarm to be raised in the town.

They were approaching the opposite zone, when they began to observe symptoms of restlessness. Some shadows moved quickly upwards, and soon after they discovered Agnes's den, brightly lit.

At the door there was a confused and compact mass struggling to peer inside. Someone must be holding her back, because despite the size of the place, it was not allowing them to pass.

Fritt drew his revolver and glanced up. Small groups were approaching the door and, advancing, said to Stuart:

"Go. The safest thing is that they will try to prevent us from entering, but if they do, we will shoot our way.

Stuart, without hesitation, came to his side with the colt in hand, and in a compact group they reached the door.

Some of his men, revolvers drawn, had planted themselves to one side of the revolving door, threatening those struggling to enter. Fritt began to elbow his way to win the door after giving Frank an order.

"When we get close, we will eliminate those two guys.

"They are 'the Cross-eyed' and 'Six Fingers'," pointed out Frank.

"As if they are the devil himself. Better.

They advanced further. The light from the lamps hanging from the door denounced them. "Six Fingers," upon discovering them, made a gesture and seemed to hesitate for a moment, but did not have time to react. Four shots vibrated and he and his partner disappeared behind the rotating blade as if sucked into thin air.

Fritt jumped on the door, commanding:

"Clear all this, soon!

But the shots were more effective than the order. The fall of the two undesirables and the presence of Fritt were enough to put them to flight. There they only breathed the airs of death and their curiosity did not reach the point of the useless sacrifice.

The entrance was cleared as if by enchantment as Fritt, Stuart and Frank and their companion jumped inside, passing over the bodies of the two fallen. Upon entering, they observed that the premises had been cleared of customers and that only half a dozen men belonging to Foot's gang were in it, the rest were upstairs.

The shots had forced them to focus their gaze on the door, at the moment when the four Dauntless leaped like tigers to gain the interior.

They saw them throw themselves on the nearest tables, throwing them to the ground and covering themselves with them, at the moment in which the rest of the gang tried to rush into the premises.

They fired furiously at the door. Someone howled in pain as they chewed lead, and a heavy volley thundered the joint. Fritt and his three companions, entrenched behind the tables, fired in turn looking for their enemies and although some of them tried to take good cover behind their makeshift parapets, three of them were hit before they could take cover and fell in the center of the room, shot at gunshots.

The other three fired furiously, but without being able to fix their aim, because it was deadly to poke their heads over the edges of the hard boards, where the projectiles stuck as well as stingers, and for a moment the barking of the colts vibrated gloomily, producing a terrible roar.

Until nervous and tense men began to appear at the top of the gallery with their weapons drawn. The bulk of the gang had gathered in Agnes's rooms, where Foot's body was located, and the roar of detonations warned them that something unforeseen was taking place below.

Soon, voices announcing the presence of Fritt's gang, gathered everyone, and like wild animals they flocked to the gallery to defend themselves and face the new enemy. A terrible fight broke out between those below protected with tables and columns and those above tried to prevent the assault.

Those attacked, sheltered behind the verandah, shot downward looking for their rivals and they raided the gallery with more advantage, since the protection that the balustrade offered them was weaker and more vulnerable.

From time to time, a groan, a curse, or a scream of death announced the well-targeted impacts. There was nothing they could try from there if they did not make up their minds to reach the hall and sweep away their enemies.

Suddenly Agnes, wearing a striking evening gown and glittering jewels, appeared in the gallery with two revolvers drawn. Magnificent and brave she came to cheer up Foot's men and force them into the fight.

"Go ahead if you are as brave as you presume! "Screamed." This can only be the work of that pig Stuart who sold you all. Where are you, traitorous pig? Why don't you show your face like men?

Some bullets tragically brushed past her. Fritt, certain that she would be killed, stuck his head in grave exposition of his life and shouted:

"Get out of there, Agnes. Nothing goes with you.

"Are you there, traitorous dog? "Roared." I should have figured it out.

"Go away," Fritt yelled, leaning out again.

She, in response, shot him. One of the projectiles grazed his hair, nearly blowing his head off. Fritt, furious, headed for her, but Stuart hit him on the arm, saying:

"Don't do that, Fritt, it's a woman.

"That almost killed me, the idiot.

But Stuart's attempt was useless.

In the barrage of intersecting bullets, Agnes was tragically struck, and, bending over on the veranda, she slipped out of it, dropped her weapons, and fell from behind like a pretty doll.

Foot's men, seeing her fall, felt a moment of discouragement, but, reacting, they threw themselves fiercely down the stairs. The fight had to be decided and from such a fragile position they could achieve nothing.

But half remained on the ladder. One by one, they fired at their enemies, causing some casualties, but the fighting was already very uneven, and the less daring fell back, disappearing down the gallery.

By the time the battle ceased and Fritt coldly counted, twelve enemies had bitten the dust.

He had lost two and had three serious injuries.

Stuart looked at Agnes with compassion rather than anger and decided not to touch anything she was wearing.

"I only have one word, Stuart. You have given me what I wanted and it is only fair that I pay. Come with me and we will settle this matter, but on the condition that you leave San Francisco at dawn.

"I also have only one word. Go.

Fritt left two men in the den to tend the fallen, and with Frank and a half dozen others returned to the place where he was meeting with his crew. Already there, he ordered:

"Whiskey for everyone. We have earned it.

It did not seem that he had witnessed a massacre like that, because he was serene and smiling. They drank eagerly and then said:

"The word is word, Stuart. Here's your money.

He put his hand to his chest pulling out a bulging wallet. From her he took the amount offered and gave it to him, inviting him:

"Drink another glass to my health. Let them serve him the best. "Stuart pocketed the money and went to the bar to get a drink. As he did so, he raised his head and in the mirror, amidst the accumulation of bottles that half blocked his vision, he caught a gesture from Fritt to Frank. He nodded. But Stuart, serene and dominating, did not accuse the discovery of that expressive and tragic gesture for his safety. He thanked the treat and offered his hand to the gunman.

"May you be lucky and earn a lot of money," he said. I hope you remember me sometime.

"Of course I will remember him. I do not forget the living or the dead "was the enigmatic answer.

"The same thing happens to me.

"When are you going?

"Tomorrow morning. Today is late and I am tired.

"Well, have a good trip and good luck.

Stuart left the joint and stepped out onto the shadowy driveway. Instinct told him that great danger was lurking and he had to control it. With fewer people around he would have wiped out Fritt as a traitor, but trying there would have been suicidal.

He took a deep look around and discovered the shadow of a nearby Tejavana. He crossed quickly, grabbed the wooden crossbar and with the agility of an ape won the roof.

Although in a precarious situation, he was able to lie on it and wait. Shortly afterwards, furtively, he saw Frank and three other gunmen come out, sticking to the facades to go unnoticed.

They searched the street without discovering him. Surprised, they went out to the center of the road and looked up and down without finding him.

"Rays of hell! "Cried Frank." Has the earth swallowed him up?

"He must have run," said one. " He would be afraid that we cleaned his money.

"We will clean it up anyway. If you have not yet arrived at the inn, we will wait for you to enter and if not ... to leave, for that matter.

They disappeared up the road. Stuart, without moving from his observatory, waited.

Half an hour later, Fritt left the joint with two of his men. Stuart heard him say:

"I'm going to bed because I'm tired. I guess Frank managed to catch that guy. The ten thousand dollars will be shared tomorrow.

"Shall we accompany you, boss?

"Do not. The danger has passed. From this moment we are the masters. Tomorrow you will tell me how it all ended.

One of his men replied:

"Do you think we end the evening at the Vanity?

"We will start spending on account of those ten thousand dollars.

The proposal accepted, they continued with Fritt up the street, but thirty yards away they separated from him to enter another establishment. Fritt looked around each other and, observing the august solitude of the street, continued on his way.

Stuart, always smiling, descended from the tejavana and, glued to the facades, walked behind the gunman. He was willing to take a hard job before he fled.

Fritt left the street of San Francisco and entered one side, then went to another parallel to the crowded road and again reached a narrower one.

Stuart, like a feline, had followed him, closing the distance until, when he reached that alley, believing that it was the right place for his plans, he decided to act coldly.

He left the protection of the houses and jumped into the dust of the road. Fritt, twelve yards ahead, was going to reach the projection of a square of light coming from a little tavern still open at such hours and when he entered the light opening, Stuart called him:

Fritt. I'm here to kill you for a traitor.

The gunman scrambled with his revolver, trying to hide the body from the light, but he didn't have time. A shot vibrated and the missile hit him in the chest. He stumbled several times and fell to the ground. Stuart ran up to him, revolver in hand, and came over.

Fritt had fallen face to face into the starry sky and was panting. Stuart quickly reached into the man's jacket pocket and pulled out the bulging wallet. Then he jumped into the shadow area and took off at a speedy run.

When the tavern patrons decided to go out and see what had happened, Fritt's body writhed in the convulsions of death. No one could see who had killed him or where the killer had fled.

The latter, satisfied with his revenge, slipped through several alleys on his way to the hotel. He knew what would be lurking in front of him, but he had not neglected his plans to evade the ambush.

The safest thing was that the gunmen, not finding him on the way, would have found out if he had already arrived and being sure that he had not, they would be waiting for him in ambush nearby. Shooting the four of them was not a business he liked and he had to outwit them.

It all depended on how they had organized the surveillance. The hotel had at its back a stockade with a corral and a gate. He had pondered it when staying there, never neglecting to cover withdrawals. He knew the gate would be closed, but the fence was easily jumpable.

Like a cat, he cautiously advanced until he approached the back of the hotel. Once there, he breathed with ease, because apparently they did not suspect that he could penetrate that part and more so when he ignored their tragic projects towards him.

He reached the fence in one leap and shot upward. When he fell into the pen he smiled.

Things couldn't have gotten better for him. There were no more Foot, no Agnes, not even that pig Fritt, to whom he had given the hegemony of the town and wanted to pay so treacherously. His accounts were settled and he had ten thousand dollars, which was in the dead man's wallet and his own savings.

Always cautious, he gained the back service door and entered the building unobserved by the clerk on duty, who was half dozing behind the counter.

With a measured and light step, he gained the stairs and when he reached the corridor, he stopped before Betty's bedroom door hesitating. If the girl was a heavy sleeper, the call could arouse the caretaker's attention and this could harm him.

He knocked discreetly with his knuckles on the door and soon, the startled voice of the young woman asked:

"Who calls?

He, applying his mouth to the seam of the door, whispered:

"Watch out; be quiet. It's me, Stuart. Opens.

Shortly after, the young woman ushered him in, murmuring:

"Oh my God! What's going on?

Now I'll tell you. Close.

He entered the bedroom and did not let her turn on the light. They could see well in the glare of the stars that penetrated through the window.

"I thought you weren't coming, Stuart," Betty said. I was afraid that ...

"The night was not very quiet, but it was fun. I have done so many things that now I marvel at having been able to do them in such a short time. For something I like nights. The ones here in San Francisco are wonderful.

"Do you want to tell me what you have done?

"Something that some would give many thousands of dollars right now to fill my belly with lead, and I have to avoid it. Get dressed, girl, we're leaving.

"Where?

"I do not know; But I do know that we're leaving San Francisco at full throttle. There is little day left and the little that remains is what we have to take advantage of.

"So, we can't wait ...

"Do not. If you look out that outside window, you will see four guys with revolver guns waiting for me to return to the hotel to give me an eternal rest. I have jumped over the wall of the corral to outwit them. If it were those solos, I might not leave, but I have the whole Fritt band behind me.

"Fritt's? I thought that...

"Yes, because Foot's doesn't exist and neither does Foot, because I took it on myself. Later, I was forced to send Fritt to hell, but his men remain. I do not perform miracles and I know how to retreat when it is convenient to do so.

"Then...

"The San Francisco airs are not good for me right now, but don't hurry; I have been paid well. I have a pocket full of money, which is the important thing.

"We will go to San Antonio or another place and set up a gambling den. We will be the owners and earn a lot of dollars.

"Why a gambling den? I would like more the peace of a ranch or a farm. I don't like this life, Stuart, and if you, if you ... really love me ... you shouldn't expose yourself to more, since you have something to live with.

"Would you really like that, dove?

"I tell you how I am sorry, Stuart.

"Good dear. We will discuss it. You ready?

"Whenever you want.

"Take the most accurate for the trip and leave the rest. We can't carry a lot of cargo.

She obeyed and with his hand they went out into the hall.

He led her to the corral. He chose the best horse he found in it, and led him out into the alley.

Already in it, he took Betty in his arms and suspended her in the air. For a few seconds he stared at her, and without putting her on the chair asked:

"Would you really like to live on a ranch?

"I swear it by the love I have for you.

"Well, you win, little one; kiss Me.

She kissed him passionately and he sat her on the chair.

Going around the corner, he reached the exit of the city. The moon reflected off the sea with silver radiations and Stuart gazed out at the poetic landscape, muttering:

"The truth is that one cannot explain such a sweet and kind place for the most sinister city in America to have been established there. If I had power, I would sink San Francisco with an earthquake and set it on fire to purify it.

And singing in a low voice a cowgirl song, he put the horse at a gallop, while on his chest he felt the soft contact of Betty's back and on his face the soft touch of her golden hair.

END